A BLAM! NOIR PULP DIME NOVELLA SERIES
BUCK ROGERS IN THE 25TH CENTURY®
DRACONIAN FIRE

blamventures.com

A BLAM! Ventures™ Production
*A BLAM! Noir™ and Retrograde™ release
of a Dime Novella™ presentation*

*Creative Direction and Written by Andrew E.C. Gaska
Cover painting by Frank Bolle and Al McWilliams
Cover design by Andrew E.C. Gaska and Anna Shausanova
Logo redesign by Ella Laytham
Book design by Maria Paula Alvarez
Production Assistance by Katie Delz
Edited by Judy Glass
Marketing and Social Media Direction by Xoie Tyler Anne Reinstein*

Buck Rogers *and* Buck Rogers in the 25th Century® © *and* ®
*1979-1981 and 2016 Dille Family Trust and are used under license.
All Rights Reserved.
Published by BLAM! Ventures, LLC.*

Second Edition. First Printing, January 2016

10 9 8 7 6 5 4 3 2 1

*No part of this book may be reproduced in any form without written
permission from the publisher.*

*All characters appearing in this work are fictitious. Any resemblance
to real persons, living or dead, is purely coincidental.*

*BLAM! Ventures LLC
P.O. Box 236
New York, NY, 10159 USA
blamventures.com*

Lo, the Rings of SATURN

DRACONIAN FIRE: EPISODE 1

ANDREW E.C. GASKA

For Adrien...

TEASER

*T*he Earth was dying.
Not all at once. Not this time.
Slowly.

Long ago, scientists had discovered that the key to life was in the food chain—the larger animals ate the smaller ones, who in turn ate smaller and smaller organisms. When it got right down to it, the tiniest of creatures were the base of the food chain, and were responsible for all life on Earth.

Disrupt that base, and the entire ecology goes out of sync.

When they blew up their world in a nuclear holocaust, 20th century man had done just that.

For 500 years, man has struggled to bring life back to Earth. It has been an uphill battle. The severe damage wrought on the planet had left it with a depleted atmosphere requiring *oxygen replenishment every several decades. Furthermore, the wholesale destruction of so many ecosystems had caused microorganisms to become endangered—including a very important strain known as Archaea. Extremophiles, the miniscule Archaea were found to inhabit nearly everywhere on Earth, including the most hostile of environments where life was thought impossible. However, even extremophiles have their limits, it seems—and they had been mostly wiped out in the holocaust. The ones who survived had a problem—the law of diminishing returns. After a few generations, they would stop reproducing. Without them, it seemed Earth's ecosystem was doomed.*

Until a new supply of Archaea was found.

Not on Earth.

Instead, the microorganisms were discovered on a moon of Saturn, of all places.

An icy blue ball called Enceladus.

Deep beneath kilometers of ice, in subterranean oceans hidden within the moon's mantle, life thrived.

Micro-life.

The same life as on Earth.

Whether it got here from there, or went there from here, didn't really matter. What did matter was that there was Earth-life on another world.

That Earth had a second chance.

Drilling through kilometers of ice and blasting through layers of solid rock, a method was devised to breach the subterranean seas of Enceladus and transport the Archaea-laden waters safely to Earth. The mining process proved so dangerous that mankind turned to their robotic prodigy—ambuquads and drones—to do the dirty work.

At last, the microorganisms in Earth's ecosystem finally seemed to be approaching sustainable levels. But the latest shipments of Archaea from Saturn were late—over half a year late. If delays continued, Earth's fragile ecosystem would begin to stray off balance yet again. When queried, the only responses from the harvesting operation were repeated requests for more security personnel and more time. Someone had to go to Enceladus and check up on the operation, find out what the problem was and fix it. Someone with the skills to infiltrate the bureaucracy running the show, turn it on its ear, and get to the root of the problem in as little time as possible. Someone with a knack for finding trouble, and causing it.

Luckily, global disaster wasn't the only thing Earth had inherited from the 20th Century.

That's where Buck Rogers came in.

***

Cobalt blasts flashed in the shadow of a giant.

As sudden death sizzled across their bow, Buck Rogers and Wilma Deering found themselves flying blind in an antique starship—stalked by a predator.

Throwing their beat-up old *Canarious* freighter into a dive, Buck plunged it right into Saturn's ring below them. The ship's hull was pelted by a million snowballs and reverberated with the peppering of tiny rocks. The battered transport tug's screens held, deflecting most of the debris. As they passed through the ventral side of the ring's debris field and into the clear, Buck immediately cut off the running lights and jinked to the right—bringing the tug back up through the Cassini Division—the dark void that separates Saturn's inner and outer rings. Unaccustomed to a cargo ship maneuvering that quickly, the enemy pilot overshot them above the ring and lost them, allowing Buck to come up around in a wide arc and settle in right behind him.

The hull moaned as the transport tug shuttered through maneuvers she was never built to achieve.

"Wilma," Buck said through gritted teeth, "I'm going to put us up right on his six. You'll get one shot."

"Roger." By now accustomed to at least some of Buck's archaic references, she had started using them herself. She flipped up the safety cover of the firing switch. Soon she was tracking their adversary, taking aim with the *Canarious's* small defensive lasers. Flying blind without any sensor signals, she would have to "eyeball it"—as Buck would say.

"Heads up!" Buck shouted.

Wilma's fingers tightened around the firing grips. As they came up fast on the enemy fighter's twin afterburners, she instantly knew something was wrong—terribly, terribly wrong!

One glance at Buck confirmed he saw it, too.

How did this happen?

The year is 1987, and NASA launches the last of America's deep space probes. In a freak mishap, Ranger 3 and its pilot, Captain William "Buck" Rogers, are blown out of their trajectory into an orbit which freezes his life support systems, and returns Buck Rogers to Earth 500 years later...

DRACONIAN FIRE: EPISODE 1

Part I

It hadn't started anything like that crazy stuff, you know—all that shooting lasers and flying starships in loop de loops.

I mean, sure, it gets there. But it starts as something a little more subdued.
Relaxed.
More like this...

ACT I

Shimmering rainbows danced before them.
Sunlight bounced off a billion ice particles, skipping off the planet's rings before cascading through them and refracting into the full spectrum of light.

One point four billion kilometers from Earth—a mere hop, skip and a jump for 25th century technology—Captain Buck Rogers and Colonel Wilma Deering settled into orbit around Saturn. The hammer-headed face of their transport shuttle was silhouetted against the bands of muted vermillion, umber and gray that washed over its hazy pale surface. There was little open space to be seen, as the huge bulk of the planet dominated everything. Wilma aligned their tiny vessel in an elliptical route directly above Saturn's outer rings and took a leisurely arc around the immense planet, admiring the view.

Chasing rainbows, Buck smiled.

Their ship was *Canarious* class—a shuttle used as a combination transport/tug. Mostly a space-going shoebox, the *Canarious* was differentiated from standard shuttles by its bow extensions and its two short ventral stabilizing fins. In use for half a century, the design was in essence the outdated workhorse of the Federated Worlds. To Buck, with its distinctive forward curved head that exceeded the width of its body, it resembled a squat hammerhead shark, minus the sleekness and finesse of any such animal.

As a light on the instrument console began to flash, Wilma updated their status.

"Sublight orbital approach is set. ETA Enceladus in forty-seven minutes."

"You know, Wilma," Buck chimed in, "sometimes I forget just how beautiful this universe is—even in our own backyard."

Wilma beamed.

After almost being trapped in another reality entirely, they were both glad to be back. Traveling a space warp to an alternate universe, Buck, Wilma, Drs. Huer and Theopolis, and Twiki, along with an escort fighter squadron, had joined forces with Princess Ardala and Commander Kane to stop an invasion.

The peaceful world of Pendar had lured them to its defense against the Warwitch Zarina and her Zaad battlecruiser. If they didn't help, the Pendarans would not grant them the ability to return home. Luckily, Buck had convinced Ardala to work with the Terrans, and together they had prevailed against the Zaad forces.

To Buck, at least, it looked as if the Princess had actually learned a lesson about how to get what she wanted without betraying everyone around her. It had marked the first true collaboration between the Draconians and Earth—something that Buck hoped would be just the first of many.

If, he lamented, *Ardala stays on course, and can talk her daddy Emperor Draco into being more reasonable.*

He scowled. A big if.

If wishes were horses.

Unfortunately, upon returning from Pendar's dimension and their uneasy alliance with the Draconians, Dr. Huer was forced to ask Buck and Wilma to go undercover immediately to see why shipments of the Archaea microorganism were being delayed from Saturn.

Buck had been out this way before, when the inner city's environmental control systems were depleted of the filtering compound Arzone 12. Then they had travelled to Titan to collect the element, and discovered the alien Garans from Vestje 4 were also in need of it to survive. A trade agreement had been formed and Earth had gained a new ally. Today, automated refineries on Titan's surface processed the Arzone for transport to both worlds.

First Arzone, then Archaea, Buck reflected. Saturn's moons, it seemed, contained many of the secrets of life itself.

Passing through another light show, Buck unconsciously ran his fingers over the rainbow-hued fabric of his uniform's armband. Instead of the usual white of the Defense Directorate, he and Wilma wore the muted purple-gray of the Security Directorate this time around. The armband, however, was the same. Emblazoned with the symbol of the Earth Government, the band itself represented more than that—so much more. Mankind had adopted the rainbow in the 25th Century to symbolize at first a unified Earth, and later a unification of all mankind throughout her former colonies. The rainbow itself represented the entire spectrum of human life amongst the stars—all equal, all united as one. Dr. Huer had shared his dream with Buck that one day it would not only include humans, but all species out amongst the stars, working together in peace. It was a goal worth being proud of, and one for which Buck commended the men of this century—men like Huer—for striving to achieve. Unfortunately, not everyone thought that way—which is why Buck and Wilma were there to 'do what they do.'

As they rounded Saturn's mass, a shadowed asteroid beyond the rings passed between the Sun and their shuttle.

Wilma regarded it. "See that artificial asteroid near Titan? A few years ago the computer council voted to increase ambuquad and drone production by building a new space station facility dedicated to it. That's *Automia*."

Buck squinted, shielding his eyes from the solar glare. Of course, the polarized viewport was already doing much of the work, otherwise Buck and Wilma might go blind if they stared too long into a star, the occasional super nova, or an exploding Draconian Marauder. To Buck, however, the computer was always a tad bit too slow in adjusting things to his comfort level.

Sometimes the old ways are the best ways.

Pinpoints of light dotted the metal asteroid's surface as lines of transport shuttles ferried supplies back and forth.

"Why out here?" Buck queried. "I mean, why Saturn?"

"Putting the facility in Saturn's orbit allows us to take advantage of the rich ore deposits in its moon system. The construction facilities on *Automia* are mostly automated, run by quads and drones with a limited rotating human staff."

Wilma continued. "Most ambuquad construction's been shifted there now, with former hubs like New Chicago and Theta Station being transformed into repair and upgrade stations instead. The computer council makes frequent visits to *Automia* and has even considered setting up there permanently," she added.

So Automia was a robot's home away from home.

Buck smiled again. *Should have called it Robotopia.*

All of the solar system's environmental issues were under the purview of the Science Directorate—and ultimately run by the computer council. Composed of a dozen limbless quad computer disks like Dr. Theopolis, the council had long ago been appointed to fix the damage mankind had made to its own environment. They had slowly brought the Earth back from extinction over the past three hundred years, and appointed their own kind to carry out their edicts.

From Huer's briefings, Buck knew the task of harvesting the Archaea had been assigned to a Dr. Maximus. The doctor was a quad who was on the fast track to becoming a member of the computer council itself. Instead of explaining why his shipments of Archaea were delayed, however, Maximus had requested additional security forces for the Enceladus harvesting site.

But with Automia hanging right around the same planet, Buck mused, why put in a call to the Security Directorate on Earth? Why not just call Automia and have the computer council send additional security androids?

Whatever problems Maximus is having out here, Buck determined, *he's trying to keep it quiet even with his own kind.*

Nevertheless, Buck and Wilma were bringing what he had asked for—just not as much of it.

While Maximus had requested ninety-six security officers, the transport tug's cargo bay had been converted to transport a division of twenty-four—low level police that were not associated with the Defense Directorate. Not a single one of them knew that there was any kind of covert operation taking place. Huer didn't want to risk a political debacle if the Science Directorate realized they were being spied on, so Buck was to be the only infiltrator. Buck and Wilma both had a subcutaneous transceiver/receiver implanted on their right cheekbones, so as long as they were within range of each other, they could talk. Wilma was to act as a pilot only, fly the *Canarious* there and drop off Rogers and the security team—then take it to Saturn's far side as backup in case Buck ran into trouble.

For *when* Buck ran into trouble.

The cockpit door pinged, sliding open behind them. Buck glanced back to see a lovely sight—Security Directive Marshall Uma Terrol. Athletic-bodied, cinnamon-haired and green-eyed, Uma's fair, freckled beauty concealed a fierceness and temper that Buck considered a rarity in this century. He had hoped he would get a chance to spend more alone time with the security expert on this trip, but realized he had to tread lightly. While Buck was undercover as the team's tactical leader, Uma was the field commander of the security forces they were bringing along. Like the rest of the troop, she had no idea of their covert mission. Buck and Wilma were completely incognito on this one—and completely on their own.

Buck spoke first. "Uma! Uh, Marshall Terrol. What brings you to this neck of the woods?"

Wilma rolled her eyes. The Marshall blinked, subconsciously reaching towards her own throat. "Woods?"

"Yeah," Buck sighed. "Forget it. What can we do for you?"

The Marshall stood at attention, all business. "Requesting an updated arrival time. I wanted to make sure the squad was prepared for debarkation."

"ETA Enceladus," Wilma punched some codes into her console, "thirty-one minutes."

The lovely Marshall nodded and turned to leave. Buck watched her saunter away, his eyes apparently lingering a little too long for Wilma's tastes.

"Now there goes a directive I can really get behind," he muttered to himself.

WHAM!

Wilma had slammed her fist down on the console in front her.

Hard.

Buck was stunned. "Wilma, I—"

"Buck Rogers," she snapped. "I *don't* want to talk about it."

Buck squirmed in his seat. "Okay, Wilma, so..." he decided to change tactics.

"What *do* you want to talk about?" He demanded. Buck turned his back to her, staring out the side viewport. Suddenly, a distant point of light was extremely interesting to him.

"Did you want to talk about..." Buck paused, glancing over his shoulder back at Wilma, not believing he was willing to fly through this stargate, "...us?"

Wilma blinked twice, then sighed.

"I suppose the real question is," she countered, staring straight ahead at the stars, "...is there an 'us'?"

Buck often wondered the same thing. It was a question neither one of them was really ready to tackle.

Not yet.

As their orbit put Saturn between them and the sun, they slipped silently into darkness.

"Passing the terminator into night," Wilma said, flicking on the *Canarious's* running lights. With no sun to shine, Saturn's darkside devoured them. The malevolent ringed giant was so colossal that it blocked out everything. Now there were no stars, only pitch black and the meager light their small ship generated. Before them, the icy sludge of the rings themselves glowed in the tug's beams, reminding Buck of a winter hunting trip he took with his dad when he was twelve. Deep in the forest on a moonless night, the only light then had been the soft purple-white glow of the luminescent snow. It was at once both terrifying and exhilarating.

Wrestling himself back to the present, Buck decided to try once more to shed some more illumination on the mission at hand.

"So what do you think's going on here, Wilma? Why the request for a security force?"

"I can only guess because of pirate activity."

"Pirates again? You don't think Ardala—"

"I honestly don't know, Buck," Wilma sighed. "But pirates are really the only thing that makes sense. The explosives they are using to penetrate Enceladus's mantle can fetch a high price on the black market. It's possible Dr. Maximus and the harvesting team have suffered many losses from raids and are trying to cover it up."

She considered any other options, and found none. "Otherwise there's no need for security at the harvesting site—it's completely automated and run by maintenance androids and ambuquads."

"Completely automated." Buck repeated. *Like Automia. And Titan.* Buck was beginning to see a trend in orbit around Saturn.

Wilma didn't seem to notice his comment. "And the detention center shouldn't be a problem, either."

"Whoa, detention center?" Buck took notice. "You mean there's a prison out here?"

"For lack of a better term, yes—on Enceladus itself. But our detention facilities aren't anything like what you had in the 20th century."

Buck scowled. "Wilma, I've been locked up a few times in this century already."

"Yes, but by other governments. Only once was in a Terran facility, and that was because we were trying to figure out exactly where you came from."

"And what pirates I was working for." he smiled. *When you thought I might be a spy sent to sabotage the treaty between the Draconian Empire and Earth.*

"Agreed." Wilma returned his smile.

"Buck, my point is that Enceladus is a long term rehabilitation facility. Every day detainees receive the latest psychological treatments via the O.E.I."

O.E.I.

Optical Engram Imager.

Buck had used it a few times—it had been useful in shifting through his memories to try to figure out who was responsible for an alleged threat to the Earth that instead turned out to be a Happy New Year's gift from their friend, Heironimus Fox.

They'd also used it to get information out of criminals who refused to talk, and it had not damaged them in any way. The same device, however, had almost been used to erase part of his memories the first time he visited New Detroit—something that never sat well with Buck.

"So waitaminute," Buck's whizzing questions all collided at once. "Is the detention center automated too? Are they reprogramming these criminals? Taking away their identity with that machine?"

"No," Wilma chuckled. "Buck, the center is staffed by both quad and human psychologists. And while the O.E.I. could—in the wrong hands—be used for such purposes, you've got to remember we are a little more civilized than that," she explained. "The psychiatric personnel use the O.E.I to go into a criminal's psyche, identify the cause of their abhorrent behavior, and create solutions for working those issues out on a subconscious level, removing the need for their negative activities."

Buck shook his head. "That all *sounds* well and good, but in my experience? No matter what the century, there's always someone ready to abuse their power. Who would want anyone messing around in their head like that?"

When Wilma didn't respond, Buck realized he was in danger of sounding like a cranky old man. Again. He decided to shift the topic. "So, who's in this prison, exactly?"

Wilma sighed again. "Rehabilitation center." Buck said it along with her, flashing her his lopsided grin.

Again she returned his smile as she considered his question. "Well, it would be any number of political enemies, spies, high profile criminals—"

Buck cut her off. "Hold on now, are you telling me that the prison on the moon we are going to is full of the people that you and I have put away over the last year and half?"

"Well, yes, I guess so. I hadn't thought of it that way."

Buck gave her a stare.

"Buck, we aren't even going to see the rehabilitation center. And even if we did, most of the detainees would be unconscious in stasis tubes or undergoing O.E.I. treatment."

Stasis tubes. "The price of progress, I suppose," Buck sighed under his breath.

The console in front of them flashed for attention. "Look's like we've reached the coordinates." Buck aligned the transmission antenna and nodded to Wilma.

"Showtime," he added.

Wilma adjusted the channel on her headset. "Enceladus Harvest Control, this is transport tug GAL 0347 on approach from New Detroit. Our cargo is the requested security force for maintaining the integrity of the harvest site. We are carrying proper admission codes and are standing by to transmit."

After a long pause, Wilma shook her head. "Strange."

Buck was making himself busy with landing prechecks. "What is it?"

"I'm not picking up anything…" she said, going over the

comm board one more time. "No return signal, and not even any comm static from Saturn itself." She pondered a moment. "It's almost like we're being—"

They both said it at the same time. "—jammed."

Buck and Wilma blinked, then both started powering up the cargo tug's defense screens.

The blasts came a second too late, refracting off their forward shields as a flash of light fired on them and blurred past the viewport. They were momentarily blinded before the smart viewport could adjust to the sudden pulsar bursts in the blackness of the darkside. There was no sensor contact—no warning. Whatever was jamming them was powerful enough to affect scanners too. Wilma opened a comm to the rear cabin and ordered Uma and her force to strap themselves in. Through the spots in his eyes, Buck double checked his equipment. Even though there was no movement on his scopes, he knew that whoever was after them was likely to be looping back around from behind for the kill. *But with jammers that powerful in play...*

If Buck and Wilma were lucky, the attackers would be sensor blind, too.

Alright, he determined. *We'll do this the old-fashioned way.*

Buck Rogers took control.

***

Plunging the freighter into Saturn's rings, Buck pulled the classic little maneuver we started this story with—dropping through the gas giant's orbiting chaos, turning off the transport tug's running lights, and shooting back up through the dark void between the inner and outer debris fields to fall in directly behind their attacker.

But you remember this part from the beginning of this story, don't you? You were paying attention, right?

I thought so.

***

"Wilma," Buck said through gritted teeth, "I'm going to put us up right on his six. You'll get one shot."

Wilma flipped up the safety cover of the firing switch. Soon she was tracking their adversary, taking aim with the *Canarious's* small defensive lasers. They weren't much, but at close range they should at least disable a starfighter.

"Heads up!" Buck shouted.

Two pinpoints of blue-white light quickly grew before them—the enemy starfighter's aft thrusters. They were coming up right behind her now. The confused starfighter had slowed down enough for them to get a look at her in the afterglow of her own engines. It was—

The fighter was *Thunder* class.

It was an Earth ship, the same as Buck and Wilma flew for the Defense Directorate. Only this one had Saturn Defense markings, and crimson ventral wings signifying a starfighter assigned to patrol a detention center.

Wilma's thumb hesitated for an instant, hovering over the firing stub.

The instant passed; she didn't get a second one.

Light erupted around them from above as they were engulfed in the telltale green aura of a tractor beam. A larger ship—a cruiser of some kind, had maneuvered in above them.

It was a trap.

"I'm sorry, Buck."

"No, I saw it too, Wilma." *Saturn Defense Force. Assigned to guard the pris—rehabilitation facility—on Enceladus.* That starfighter was supposed to be on their side. *Was this just a case of mistaken identity?* he pondered.

As the tractor beam rendered the controls useless, Buck threw his hands up in the air in a gesture of frustration and dropped them to his lap. Now he realized why the starfighter had slowed so much; they had been herded towards the cruiser for just this purpose. *Clever*, Buck conceded. *Not your run-of-the-mill 25th Century strategist.* Whoever their opponents were—be they friend or foe—Buck and Wilma were now theirs.

ACT II

Lightning arced across the stars.

In the Gamma Draconis system, four distant shimmering points seemed to spiral and pulse in a diamond formation. Three horizontal bursts of light erupted as the energies of faraway solar bodies were directed and focused through stationary refractor satellites. For the briefest of moments, the space between them was warped—the immense gravity of those stars bending space to the will of their caller, and opening a glowing door to another part of the galaxy. The portal appeared to be split vertically down the middle, forming two distinct, separate places, joining here and there together.

A kilometers-long mechanical behemoth appeared within the discharge barrier, crossing a threshold of a hundred light years in a matter of seconds. Bristling with gun turrets and launch tubes, massive contratureen reactors and missile bays, the monstrous warship finally emerged from the stargate. Their task accomplished, the stars flashed once again in unison and seemed to die out, the satellites no longer channeling their immense power.

Now, on final approach to the planet Gamma Draconis III, in what from Earth would be seen as the Constellation of Draco, the *Draconia* had come home.

Well, at least, this *Draconia* had.

She was in fact the second ship to bear the name, something that the citizens and soldiers of the realm were not told about. Laden with warheads and weapons, the original *Draconia* had served the Emperor for decades, often being refit and updated with the latest equipment. She had served as the vanguard of many an invasion under the command of King Draco himself. That was until she was stripped of all outside armament and Princess Ardala was given control of her.

In the ill-fated invasion that had inadvertently introduced Buck Rogers to the 25th Century, Ardala and Killer Kane had lost the original *Draconia* in a fierce battle with Earth forces.

Ardala had placed the blame squarely on Killer Kane's shoulders, and thus had escaped her father's wrath. 'Killer' had not been so lucky.

As for the *Draconia*...

It was simply unacceptable that the *Draconia* had been destroyed fighting the Terrans: the people of the empire need only hear of the realm's successes, not its failures. The official statement suggested that while the *Draconia* faced severe weapons' fire as well as internal sabotage from the untrustworthy Earthers, the ship still triumphed in the end.

To perpetuate the lie, all crew that abandoned their posts in fear via escape pods were rounded up and summarily executed and/or banished.

All, of course, save for the Princess.

The remaining crew that had stayed aboard the first *Draconia* and defended her honor were commended.

Posthumously.

And so Draco went about replacing his flagship. He ordered the newest ship of the fleet, the *Rastaban,* to simply *disappear*. The ship's navigation control was locked on a course for a stargate, and her engines simulated a meltdown. This crew escaped in lifeboats as well, but were reassigned. The *Rastaban* disappeared through the stargate and emerged right into the tractor beam of a hidden Draconian shipyard facility. Those unlucky enough to stay at their posts until the bitter end—including her gallant captain and engineer—were executed and given a hero's funeral, their family legacy assured in the annals of Draconian history.

Now, a Draconian honor guard marched double time down the *Draconia's* main corridor, clearing the passageway of all personnel. Princess Ardala and her entourage of handmaidens and bodyguards followed, the oiled, ebony-skinned Pantherman taking up the rear.

As always, Ardala was dressed to kill. Her sheer violet-hued robe did little to conceal her bronzed skin and bejeweled undergarments. Attached behind her shoulders was a pair of large ornamental sequined wings. Composed of a memory-material, they would unfurl back to their original shape even if the Princess crushed them by sitting down while wearing them. Her costume was accentuated by her crown—an impressive diadem exclusively reserved for the first-born of Draco, heir to the throne and realm.

As they rounded the corridor leading to the hangar deck, Ardala rolled her eyes. When the newer *Draconia* has entered service, anyone who had served on both vessels would have immediately known something was amiss.

To Ardala, the old *Draconia* was an eyesore. Dark and musty, her rusty corridors creaked from the strain of countless battles. The new ship, however, had brightly colored interiors with the latest accoutrements.

Designed for a Princess.

Still, none of the new ship's crew would dare speak of it openly—to do so would mean instant death. Ardala imagined there were hushed whispers to their little women when on leave, in the dead of night, but such talk was best left to bedroom gossip, lest one wanted to find himself alone in an interrogation room with Tigerman.

There were even preposterous ghost stories circulated of the *Rastaban* haunting battlefields, as if that ship was still out there, and that her captain and chief engineer had become undead Vorvons still answering Draco's commands, attacking and devouring the life energy of all enemies of the empire.

The Princess smirked at such nonsense. No, the *Rastaban's* crew were quite dead. The ship had been quietly renamed *Draconia* and delivered once again into her hands and those of an officer named Kane—for better or for worse. And it was this Kane who awaited her at the *Draconia's* hangar deck—to serve as her yacht's pilot for the trip to Gamma Draconis's surface.

But this was not the insolent and power hungry "Killer" Arin Kane. For his part in the first earth debacle, *Killer* Kane was stricken from the records, both his existence and final fate unrecorded. No, this was his older brother, Ansara.

Commander Kane.

The mustached elder Kane was a different kind of man—a treasured advisor to her father for years. While arrogant—(a trait that evidently ran in his family line)—Ansara Kane's loyalty was unwavering, and his scientific achievements had advanced the Draconian warmachine with his improved and more deadly hatchet fighters. For over a year now he had served her well, despite his inherent flaws.

As Ardala approached the royal yacht, the honor guard split into two divisions, flanking her path to the ship's ramp. Kane stood at attention just outside the ship. Deeply vain, a characteristic he shared with the Princess, his affinity for extravagant and well-tailored vestments often outshone her fashion sense, much to her chagrin, and today's wardrobe was no different. The Commander was garbed in a jewel encrusted longcoat of supple Saurian leather over a high-collared tunic, and trousers of Alberan spider-silk, interwoven with threads of pure platinum. To Ardala, it was his most outlandish outfit yet—the collar's edge soared a good half–meter above his head—and Kane could likely only see directly ahead of him. As she approached, he extended his hand, his eyes locking with hers, then quickly glancing down and back up again.

"Princess," Commander Kane announced matter-of-factly. Apalled that he would overstep his boundaries and dare to even insinuate tactile contact, Ardala still followed his eyes down to the ramp she was standing on... to a gap between the yacht and the ramp. Not a wide one, but the two edges were clearly not flush. However unlikely, no one wanted to entertain the risk that the Princess might catch her foot on the uneven surface and stumble. She relented, raising her chin high, gingerly allowing Kane to take her hand, and stepped over the gap into the yacht.

Kane had performed perfectly. In fact, when faced with such a situation, it was indeed proper etiquette to offer one's hand to the Princess. To not do so would be grounds for termination

Regardless, she steamed, *this was inexcusable.* Whoever was responsible for this insult *must* be punished.

Ardala and her servants settled into the yacht's plush cabin as her commander proceeded to the cockpit.

"Kane," she called out, annoyed. A serving girl was already pouring her an Antarean brandy.

"Already taken care of, my Princess. The crewman who set the ramp will spend three days in detention," he paused for effect, "...where he will receive forty lashes a day from Patherman."

"Well done, Kane," she sang, downing her first glass. "Well done."

Soon, the yacht was on its way down to the surface—and to the Royal Palace of Emperor Draco himself.

***

Gamma Draconis III was a volcanic planet, covered in a haze of ashen browns and vibrant orange-reds. Ardala's yacht descended through blackened clouds of acrid smoke that obscured the planet's blazing fire pits and gladiatorial coliseums, within scintillating waves of heat.

For Ardala, it was comforting to be home. After nearly being stranded in another universe by those boorish Pendarians, the Zaad incident had turned in their favor because of the temporary alliance with the Earth Directorate. For once, she had not been at odds with Huer and Deering, and had found the experience strangely rewarding.

And then there was Buck.

She had finally come to terms with the fact that she would never have him—but maybe she didn't need to. She was strong, resilient, and had even finally proven herself in combat.

Perhaps I need no man. Ardala downed her third cocktail of the flight.

Perhaps.

Tradition clearly stated that she must find a husband to rule, but she would talk to Draco, and maybe he could change all that. He was, after all, conqueror of space, warlord of Astrium, and ruler of all the Draconian realm.

The royal yacht's soft landing in the palace hangar was in sharp contrast to the harsh environment outside it. Mt. Draconis was erupting again, rivers of lava sliding down its face like heavy, glowing, molten tears, converging in cooling lakes of fire around its base. The lava would never touch the palace itself nor its well-manicured grounds, owing to the miracle of engineering that, carefully directed all lava flow around it, through the meticulously chiseled and honed landscape. Even in the unlikely event that the volcano were to go pyroclastic, a heat resistant forcefield was in place around the palace. But still there was no need to worry, as the palace's deep sensors would alert them long ahead of time to any such catastrophe, and geo-engineers would diffuse the pressure buildup within the caldera before any serious cascade came to pass.

Glancing around the bay, she immediately noticed there were several royal yachts already secured in bays of their own. "Curious," she said aloud. Kane immediately took notice, and nodded in agreement.

As Ardala entered the palace, she knew instantly that something was wrong. The guards, she observed, all seemed nervous as they requested the Princess to proceed with only Kane and one bodyguard. She complied, knowing that her father did not like the servants intermingling. As she, Kane and Patherman made their way through the palace halls, she could hear a distant rumble—not unlike the tremors preceding a volcanic eruption. Mt. Draconis, however, was already erupting, and the palace was sound proofed against outside noises. No, the distant roar she heard must be coming from inside the palace itself. The vibrations reached their crescendo as they approached the throne room, and the guards threw open the doors for her.

It was like walking into a tidal wave.

The throne room was filled to capacity, and then some. All twenty-nine of her sisters were in attendance, all with their personal guards and adjutants—and all having very separate and very loud conversations of their own. Servants darted through the masses to and fro, bringing hors d'oeuvres and drink to anyone lucky enough to notice them. It seemed as if her entire family was holding a party, and forgot to invite her.

An oversight, I'm sure, she fumed.

Ardala and her sisters were regularly situated within their own provincial regions of space, and Draco was usually careful to make certain that no more than three were visiting the capitol at the same time. Having the daughters of Draco in the same space was dangerous—they all served only one agenda—their own. Feeling herself being watched, Ardala's eyes in turn settled on Princess Valdemara and her diminutive twin Mynx. Ardala's youngest sisters, the fraternal twins were the product of Draco's union with his forty-seventh wife Umeko—a former concubine whom he had elevated to free status and then married. Like his previous wives, including Ardala's mother, Umeko had met an untimely death at the hands of assassins striking against the Empire. Ardala's youngest siblings unnerved her. Although they bore little resemblance to each other, they were always moving in unison, always finishing each other's sentences.

Now, Valdemara and Mynx seemed to circle her like Reptovultures, their eyes penetrating her like so many daggers, all probing for a single weakness, but finding not one, she was sure.

One of them had talked their father into taking her Tigerman away from her, a personal slight Ardala had not forgotten. Her former bodyguard, Tigerman was here, apparently now part of the twins' entourage. His loyalties torn, the warrior refused to meet Ardala's eyes.

"Well," Ardala stole a look in Kane's direction and forced her words as if through steeled fangs, "it appears everyone's here."

Kane too was suspicious, and had noticed something she had not. "Not everyone, my Princess."

In a not-quite-princess-like manner while in a room full of princesses, Ardala stood on her toes, completing a quick survey on the chamber.

I've picked up Buck's bad habits. Etiquette be damned.

Kane was correct, the only living blood relative not present in the throne room seemed to be Emperor Draco himself.

All thirty daughters of the Emperor in one room, and Draco was no where to be found, she mused. *Either he is planning on locking us all in and letting us tear each other's throats out, or...*

Ardala feared the worst. *Could daddy be—*

"Princess Ardala!" the Emperor's Vizier, a thin man named Pythios, approached them. A spindly top-knotted creature with a hawkish nose, Pythios was adorned with a partial skull cap, voluminous robes, and a curling reddish goatee. Ardala had never trusted him growing up; the man was as slippery as his namesake.

"Ah, Your Grace," he proclaimed, bowing courteously. "Your father has been waiting to see you." Pythios' gaunt face looked up at Commander Kane. "Alone."

Kane stiffened.

"Need I remind you, Vizier, that I am the Emperor's Minister of Planetary Affairs?"

The Vizier properly demonstrated his subservience.

"Forgive me, Commander. These orders come from Emperor Draco himself."

The Commander acquiesced, motioning Pantherman to stay as well. The Princess barely noticed.

Draco's alive, Ardala breathed.

The Vizier led her towards the Emperor's personal chambers. "Please, this way."

***

"You must forgive my pilot for firing on you, of course," the glowing blue disk exclaimed.

Buck Rogers and Wilma Deering stood before the Archaea harvesting operation's lead scientist, Dr. Maximus, on the hangar deck of the Enceladus rehabilitation picket cruiser. The guards behind the duo unlocked their magnetic cuffs, and Buck rubbed his sore wrists. Maximus was doing his best to be ingratiating, to a point where Buck was becoming uncomfortable. The computer's demeanor was simply...oily. The quad sat on an extension arm attached to a multi-armed crimson drone. The drone moved back and forth in a short line, a robot's close approximation of pacing.

As soon as they had been tractor–beamed into the carrier, the tug's cockpit had been stormed by armed security androids, while her converted cargo bay had been left locked—preventing Uma and her security officers within from offering any resistance. Buck and Wilma had been arrested, cuffed, and led out onto the hanger deck while a sensor drone confirmed their digital documentation.

Nearby, a seated scrawny man was hunched over a security console, having just finished running Buck and Wilma's identification. The man passed their IDentitags to the drone. Maximus shifted spectra to purple and continued.

"You must realize we had to be sure you really were who you said you were. We've had problems with pirates, you see—and humans can be so melodramatic. Your documentation, of course, checks out—Officer Mateo," the computer disk commented as the drone handed Buck back his IDentitag, "...and Pilot Dex," he completed, as Wilma was handed hers. They had passed the first big hurdle; their identities were not compromised.

As Uma and the rest of the security officers Buck and Wilma had brought were released from the cargo bay, Maximus counted them. "...23, 24." Maximus indicated Buck. "Plus you makes twenty-five men. I am curious, however, why there is only one quarter of the force I ordered."

Ordered, not requested, Buck noted. He spoke up first.

"We, ah, we're the advance team!" Buck clasped his hands behind his back and began to pace in sync with the drone carrying Maximus. "Yeah, you know, New Detroit just couldn't put together the full complement at once, so they sent us ahead instead of leaving you with no protection at all."

Buck smiled.

"I see." Maximus's light patterned face dimmed somewhat, appearing to form a frown.

Feeling confident in Buck's answer, Wilma pressed the issue. "In fact, Doctor, by the time I get back, the second division should be ready, and I'll just ferry them right along here." She smiled as well.

Dr. Maximus's color turned a sour greenish-yellow.

"Get back?" he queried. "Oh, no, my dear—oh, no. You're not going anywhere. You've arrived just in time—the big operation is today! I am short a shuttle and I need everyone in the air for this—lots of cargo to move, you see!"

Dr. Maximus returned to his original blue hue as he continued. "I've read your documentation.- I need your transport tug and I need your piloting skills. I'm afraid you're needed here far more than on the shuttle circuit."

Buck stopped pacing. *Mice and Men and all that...*

Wilma paused. "Well, at least let me contact my superiors, let them know—"

Maximus's drone was already carrying him away.

"I'll talk to the science council, and get this all cleared. Until then, you can co-pilot your *Canarious* with Captain Harris—he should be prepping your ship right now."

"Right," Wilma replied. Buck shot her a wink.
The drone stopped one last time as Maximus addressed Buck.
"Something wrong with your ocular cavity, Mateo?"
Buck rubbed away mock tears as he shook his head.
"Me? No..." he sniffed. "Sometimes I just get a little... misty."
"...Right," Maximus replied, after a pause. "Chief Garrett will brief you and your division on your job."

Damn. Wilma doesn't get to fly home, and now they are splitting us up.

Seated at the security console nearby, a studious older man stood up. Chief Garrett was a fop of a man, effete and smallish—both in appearance and in mannerism. Instantly, Buck didn't like him. Not because of his physical attributes, but because of his snobbish arrogance. The Chief's handshake was sweaty and limp. Buck grabbed his hand like a vice, and shook heartily, meeting Garrett eye-to eye.

Garrett's carpal bones made a sound like a 20th Century breakfast cereal.

Intimidated, Garrett, looked away, managing only to stammer out, "Ow," as he withdrew his hand. As he nursed his wrist, he indicated Buck and his security team to follow him towards the security landing craft. As they walked, they talked.

"Officer Mateo," Garrett started. "I envy you."

"Oh, you do?" Now Buck was confused.

"Why, yes!" His confidence up, Garrett continued. "Not many people in this business have had the opportunity to study under me. I think you will find that my perspective of the criminal mind is very different from the usual security personnel. You see," and for this he paused and raised his head in pride, "I have three degrees in aberrant xenopsychology. I like to think of myself as more a psychiatrist than a security chief. I actually understand the mind of a criminal, so I have an edge over all of them." He turned to Buck directly and smiled. Buck's stomach turned. Garrett continued, "You are serving under the best, I assure you!"

All this, and modest, too. Buck forced a smile.
"Swell," he pushed through a wired-shut jaw.

Maximus chuckled as the ruby colored drone finally carried him off the hangar deck. "Back to work, humans!"

***

As Chief Garrett led Buck and the security force away, Wilma saw drones and men hard at work decoupling the passenger bay from the transport tug. They looked to be installing a high powered tractorbeam module in its stead. Moving past the hustle and bustle, she made her way to the cockpit.

She was ambushed before she made it to the controls.

"Hi," her new co-pilot exclaimed, looking her over from head to toe. "You must be Lieutenant Dex. I'm Captain Harris, but you," he sniffled, "you can call me Andy…"

Andy was a little young to be playing shuttle captain. Gangly and awkward with a runny nose, he looked like he had barely graduated from the academy.

Wilma tried her best to smile.

Really she did.

"Ok…" Wilma paused, eventually spitting it out. "Andy."

Captain Harris smiled and immediately went back to fiddling with the control board. He had just finished installing some kind of secondary security computer system to the ship's console, and was testing it with the remote he carried on his person. As she watched him wipe his nose on his sleeve, Wilma began to get the idea that Maximus was pulling his staff from an extremely limited pool of personnel.

As she sat in the copilot's seat beside him, she noticed that the pulsar batteries were dry. She asked Captain Har—Andy—about it.

"We pulled the packs," he replied, matter of factly.
"We can't risk weapon's fire coming from a ship carrying *our* cargo."

The board to Wilma's right lit up green; the tractor beam

module was primed and ready. Several androids wheeled a large flat conical object beneath the tug—apparently the cargo.

"Our cargo, right." Wilma turned towards him. "And that is?"

As he flipped switches, the tractor beam came to life, securing the cargo to the ship's lower hull. Harris sat back in his seat. Colored lights began to pulse down the launch tube before them. A steady thrumming gathered in crescendo as the starship catapult primed.

"All the shuttles are bringing in explosives for the mine shaft at the harvest site." He coupled his flight harness to the seat restraints. "You and me, Dex? We get to carry the detonation cap—a *blazium* warhead."

Blazium. Wilma and Buck had used it before to alter the course of a kilometers-long mass of frozen oxygen in space, allowing the so called "spaceberg" to traverse a narrow window safely into Earth's atmosphere. The most powerful explosive in the known universe, only a miniscule amount of blazium was needed for the task. A brick was said to be enough to blow up an entire moon.

That warhead is much bigger than a brick.

They are going to use it on a moon.

Before she could respond, Wilma was thrown back in her seat. The *Canarious*, with its deadly cargo, hurled toward the stars.

ACT III

"Welcome to the Enceladus Harvesting Operation!" Chief Garrett's voice cracked.

Buck Rogers's trip to the surface had been bumpy—much more so than he was accustomed to in the 25th Century. The landing craft he had ridden in was a rickety older model, way past its prime and certainly not safe to be carrying any large explosive payloads, let alone people. In fact, it somewhat resembled a refit prisoner transport.

Probably a hand-me-down from the rehabilitation center, Buck concluded. *No wonder they commandeered Wilma and the transport tug.*

They had travelled from the picket cruiser to a hangar kilometers away from the harvest crater on Enceladus. Now, Buck and the new security team were packed into an antigrav monorail car, gliding at supersonic speeds toward the site. He was seated at the head of the car, directly next to the standing Garrett. He noted with interest that Security Directive Marshall Terrol—Uma—was seated almost directly across from him, her red locks radiant in the afterglow of the speeding lights outside the rail car.

He took the opportunity to enjoy the view.

Each of them had been handed a large silver hard plastic case with their supplies in it. Curious, Buck cracked open his case to sneak a peek inside. Garrett slammed it shut, leaning in close to Buck and wagging a finger in his face.

"Don't do that," Garrett whispered urgently, holding the case shut with his other hand. "Don't jump ahead. I'm getting to that. I'm going to explain that."

Buck smiled, put the case at his feet and clasped his hands in his lap.

"Sorry."

If Dr. Huer exemplified all that was good and noble in 25th Century man, Garrett was his polar opposite: self-important where Huer was humble, ignorant where he was wise, and desperate to be followed when Huer was a natural leader.

No, Buck did not like this little man, and now there was no going back. He decided that given half a chance, he was going to give Garrett a hard time. *A very hard time.*

Garrett started his briefing.

"The area around the mining camp is covered by a low density forcefield designed to hold a heated atmosphere in. As long as everyone stays within the site's designated breathing zone, you won't lose your breath." He went on to explain that the heated nature of the zone was relative—while the moon's general surface temperature was minus 201° Celsius, the site was kept at constant a negative 10°.

Buck shivered.

"That's what your hot suit is for," Garrett continued. "Keep it on and you will keep from freezing. You will find one in your supply case."

As all the other security personnel began to open their cases,

Buck sat serenely—smiling and looking directly at Garrett. The security chief leaned over to Buck and whispered again.

"It's ok now," Garrett said, showing Buck what the others were doing. "Now you can look inside, because I mentioned it."

Buck put on a facade of confusion. He pointed to the case, looking up at Garrett inquisitively.

The dreadful little man sighed.

"Now," he mouthed.

Buck gave him a thumbs-up, and opened his case.

Examining Buck's thumb, then his own, the confused Garrett elected to continue addressing everyone instead. "Again, rebreathers are unnecessary, as long as you stay within the breathing zone. Outside the zone's forcefield there is no oxygen to breathe. Enceladus's natural atmosphere is primarily composed of water vapor and minute particles of ice." For this part Garrett cracked an ugly little smile: "Without your rebreather you would literally drown on the surface." He paused and stared directly at the men. "Now, suit up!"

The security force scrambled at once into their hot suits. As he zipped up his, Buck realized it was essentially a light spacesuit without helmet or oxygen tanks, but with environmental controls. Buck also saw there were several other goodies in the hardcase. Garrett droned on.

"Enceladus's gravity is less than a fifth of Earth's. There is no antigrav plating on the surface, only the lower levels. You will have to wear magnetic boots while not underground." He struggled to put his right foot up on the rail nearest to Buck to showcase the footwear. The effete man almost fell over. "This dial adjusts the boots' gravity, so you can either make it lighter and leap or dial it up and lock yourself in place."

"That's one way to get yourself out of a sticky situation," Buck muttered aside, "or stuck right in it."

Garrett stared inquisitively at Buck again.

Straight-faced, Garrett replied. "You are a curious individual, Officer Mateo."

Buck smiled, then stole a quick glance at Uma. He winked at her. She rolled her eyes and looked away.

Trying to process the joke, Garrett didn't notice the exchange.

After a moment, he admitted defeat. "I don't get it."

Looking back at Uma, Buck smiled again.

"Neither will I," he said.

Now ignoring Buck, Garrett explained the remaining contents of the case.

"You have been issued a short range commlink that will function only within the atmosphere shield, and a pulse pistol. Your assigned positions have been uploaded to your pocket comps. All this is designed to help you do your job more efficiently."

"Cool. What *is* the job, exactly."

Garrett simply looked at him.

"I mean, I *know* it's security. And, I know that it's for the harvesting site. But what are we securing *against*, exactly?"

"The job itself is simple," Garrett finished, "you just keep the workforce in line. They're supposed to be clearing ice, setting up barricade sheets and dampening fields for when we detonate the demolitions pit and crack the mantle open." Garrett stressed the point. "It's the only way to get to those microorganisms that Earth needs so badly."

As the antigrav train pulled into the station, the security forces stowed their empty cases under their seats, and got ready to disembark. The Chief tried in vain to be heard over the din.

"Keep them out of trouble. Keep them doing their job, and you get to keep yours," Garrett barked. "Got it?"

As an affirmative was muttered throughout the group, a confused Buck Rogers stepped up to the plate.

"Yeah, except for one thing." Buck queried. "Why would we need to keep drones in line?"

"Drones, heh!" Garrett chuckled. "Funny you should call them that."

The doors to the car slid open.

As the other officers shoved their way off the antigrav train, Buck was pushed along with them. On the platform right outside, they each stopped to adjust their boots to the low gravity, causing a pile up.

The train doors whisked shut, and Buck watched the monorail rocket away, *with Garrett still aboard.*

Little weasel doesn't even go on the site with his people.

"This is worse than the New York subway." Looking after the retreating Garrett, he continued. "We had lousy entertainment and everything. The only thing missing were the panhandlers."

Uma was kneeling next to Buck, priming her left boot's antigrav system.

She looked up at him. "Were you talking to me?"

"Not necessarily." Buck blushed, before giving orders.

"Do what they tell you to do, but also run a perimeter sweep and meet me at the center of the camp at, say..." Buck glanced at his chronometer and shook his head, still distracted by Garrett's ineptitude as a leader, "twelve hundred hours." That gave them both three hours to take in the lay of the land. "I want to know what this place's weak points are."

As she nodded in the affirmative, Buck shook his head and moved on. "I gotta stop talking to myself."

"Wait," Uma Terroll stared after him, confused.

"What's a pan-handler?"

***

"GAL 0347 has cleared launch tube and is en route to Enceladus," Wilma reluctantly reported.

The *Canarious* swept away from the picket cruiser and towards a stained ink spot against the bright backdrop of Saturn. Her explosive cargo held snug beneath her in the green tinted vice-grip of her tractor beam, the transport tug was soon flying parallel to the dark icy moon's surface, speeding towards morning.

"Control to GAL 0347. You are authorized for approach on course 387—we've got some congestion at site and won't need you right away. Enjoy the scenic route."

"Thank you, control," Wilma replied. "GAL 0347 on approach, ETA seven minutes."

The sun was beginning to peer over the horizon now, a miniscule yet dazzling spectacle. Seeing it this far away—smaller than earth's moon appears in the sky back home—and peeking out over an exceptional ice crevice in the frozen landscape—subconsciously gave Wilma the shivers. She adjusted the temperature of her pilot's suit two degrees warmer.

Captain Harris—Andy—soon pointed out glowing lights on the horizon. "Enceladus encampment coming up on visual range—"

"—now."

And what a sight it was.

Seen from above, the harvesting camp did not fail to impress. Surrounded by multiple energy fences at its perimeter and serviced by an antigrav monorail from a launch bay half a click away, the complex was laid out in a series of concentric circles. Wide avenues choked with utility pods and other makeshift construction housing ran between rings of dampening fields and permaslab barriers, gradually tightening as they spiraled their way towards the epicenter of the site. There, several cargo shuttles hovered at standby over a massive ice crater, waiting for their turn to unload their cargo. The crater itself was surrounded by a trio of gargantuan transmission towers sporting tractor beam cranes. Those cranes in turn were sending bulk loads and equipment down a mineshaft wide enough to fly a starfighter into that had been drilled directly in the crater's center. According to Wilma's sensors, that shaft ran deep—too deep for a clear reading.

Large sonic and laser drills were being extracted from the crater, their work apparently done. The entire site was enclosed in a soft forcefield designed to hold an atmosphere and a modicum of heat in.

Several personnel transport barges flew past them back up to orbit—*or were they going somewhere else?* Wilma craned her neck to watch them go.

There's something about their flight vector...

Harris took over the comm set. "GAL 0347 to control, on schedule for delivery of explosive package four seven. We are carrying the 'crust buster' payload and request a 'clear skies' protocol."

"We see you GAL 0347," Control replied, "Both workforce and security have arrived. Please assume holding pattern Alpha Jay until the other payloads are placed."

Seeing the line of cargo shuttle traffic ahead of them, Wilma realized they might be out here a while.

I hope Buck is having better luck finding out what's going on than I am.

She settled in for a long wait.

***

As he emerged onto the site's surface, Buck surveyed his surroundings. The first thing he noticed was the blue.

The blue was everywhere.

Everything on the surface on Enceladus seemed to have a bluish white tint to it. It wasn't unpleasant, not in the slightest, but it simply made you think things were just that much colder.

The second thing in abundance was the cold. It was the kind that ate at your face and ears, leaving them numb the instant you stepped out into it. He dialed up his suit's thermostat, and enjoyed the warm air blowing up his collar and over his ears.

Next was the ice; the entire moon's surface was made of it. As he walked on what was actually a frozen solid ocean, his gravity boots crunched it beneath him. Buck was walking on a wide semicircular avenue on that ice ocean, with an energy fence on the outer side, and permaslab barriers on the inner one. Three large crane towers asserted themselves against the sky nearby, standing over what he assumed could only be the drilling site. Those cranes were in turn dominated by Saturn itself, the pale glowing giant forever staring down on Enceladus, filling up two thirds of the entire sky.

Enceladus was an interesting place.

The security personnel moved en masse towards the widest part of the alley, so Buck followed suit. Scanning the crowd, he realized that he had already lost track of Uma and all the members of the team he'd brought along—there were simply too many guards here.

An alarm blared, announcing incoming transports. The more experienced guards seemed to adopt an authoritative stance which Buck found, well... amusing.

Were the robot workers supposed to find that intimidating?

Buck puffed out his chest, tucked in his chin, and did his best to ape the man nearest him.

He found the pose hard to keep.

He didn't have to keep it very long.

Four personnel transport barges soon touched down on the wide curved paved ice before them. Essentially a stripped down fighter cockpit sans the fighter, a barge's command module was connected to a lone spine and pincer apparatus that terminated aft in an engine thruster assembly. The bulk of its body was the fat six-sided personnel transport pod slung underneath, snug and secure in the pincers connected to the spine.

As the barges touched down, they disengaged their personnel pods and idly took off again, leaving the hexagonal pods lined up along the avenue. As a klaxon gave the all clear, the pod bay doors opened wide, and the robot work force began to disembark.

It was then that Buck saw them for the first time.

They appeared to be bipedal humanoid types, like the maintenance androids he'd seen in countless worker positions—including acting as security onboard Maximus's cruiser. Unlike Twiki or other ambuquads, they were given human proportions and shape to be more acceptable to mankind. Their faces were usually fake and mask-like, designed to give a semblance of human life from a distance, but quite clearly not human upon close inspection.

Except as he got closer, Buck could see these didn't look like that.

These looked like, well... people.

Disheveled, dirty, and tired people.

Buck was immediately reminded of his prison break last year on Zeta's Moon Three, and the guard android he called Hugo that had pursued him mercilessly.

The Zetans had developed androids so authentic that they could pass for human from outside appearances, although their programming was certainly not as complex as the positronic brains employed by Theo, Twiki, and their kin. Hugo was one of them.

But unlike Zeta, Earth and the Federated Worlds had a strict ban on human simulacrum androids—so if that was the case, Dr. Maximus was breaking several laws.

It wasn't the case.

Dr. Maximus was still breaking several laws, however.

Much worse ones.

A quick scan of this crowd, and Buck began to recognize faces. Rorvik from the Cornell Traeger affair, the thug Yarat he had fought with on Music World, even Koren from the Hieronymus Fox kidnapping...

They've got to be from Enceladus's rehabilitation center, he realized. *These are all prisoners.*

Inmates.

What they call in the 25th Century "Detainees."

Humans. Aliens.

Living beings.

They were the ones digging the mine shaft. They were doing the harvesting.

And from the looks of them, not by choice.

They were being using as forced labor. Essentially—

Slaves.

***

Captain Harris—A.K.A. Andy—was knuckle deep in a mining operation of his own.

Wilma suspected—hoped even—that the objective of his personal dig was not to unleash any micro-organisms.

This was an excavation, pure and simple.

As he withdrew the digit from his nose, Wilma averted

her eyes, almost certain she would rather not know what he had discovered. When she finally dared to peek anew, he was examining his results with almost fanatical interest.

Wilma interrupted.

"Um..."

As soon as she spoke, the man-boy abandoned his analysis, wiping his new specimen on the side of his flight suit.

Wilma shuddered.

"Andy," he reminded her. "Call me Andy." He smiled.

"Right, Andy." Jaw set, Wilma pressed on.

"Andy—the payload we are carrying..." she needed to be delicate here.

"Blazium." Andy Harris was now staring out the viewport at the other shuttles ahead of them, apparently already distracted again.

"Right." Wilma went for broke. "Couldn't that blow up this entire moon?"

"Well," Harris turned to look at Wilma and stopped. Instead he produced a personal calculating device from his pocket and quickly worked out some numbers. Impressed with the results, he continued.

"In theory, yes..."

Wilma sighed. Suddenly she understood how Buck must have felt talking to her on the flight to Saturn.

"Look." Harris reached forward with his clean hand and flipped a few switches on the console between them. Soon, a computer simulation of the camp, and what lay below it, appeared on the main monitor.

"This is that mining shaft the shuttles are unloading into. We've tunneled through nearly thirty kilometers of ice to get as close as possible to the subterranean ocean containing that micro-bacteria we're here to harvest," he explained.

"The Archaea," Wilma offered.

"Right, whatever they are," he snapped. "They're bugs."

Wilma noted his irritation with interest.

Contempt for the assignment, or something more?

Recovering from the interruption, Harris refocused.

"The last ten kilometers is super dense mantle containing iron and silicates, so now we have to blast."

He pointed to an ovoid chamber situated between the ice shelf and the mantle. "Right there we've dug out a demolitions den and are packing it full of shaped charges now. The den is designed to concentrate the explosives and channel them directly downward through the mantle. Then you and I go in, tractor down the blazium, and BOOM!" With that last part, he threw his hands in the air, as if to simulate an explosion.

Wilma wasn't impressed.

Harris shrugged his shoulders and sat back in his seat, nonetheless satisfied with his own performance.

"If Dr. Maximus's calculations are correct," he continued, "ten kilometers of rock will be vaporized instantly, and we will have our access to the underground sea, and those bugs Earth needs so badly."

"And if his calculations are wrong?" Wilma probed.

"He's a computer." Harris laughed. "Since when is a computer ever wrong?"

***

Buck Rogers had a date with a red headed beauty.

One who carried a gun and could kill with her bare hands.

At least, he wished he did.

He had to find Uma again, and let her know not only that the harvesting site was using an illegal prison labor force, but also who he really was.

Fact was, now Buck needed protection.

Not that kind, thank you very much.

You know what I mean.

The last thing he needed right now was the wrong felon to recognize him. This entire camp could come down on him at once for revenge.

Buck had put too many of these guys away, and it was only a matter of time before that fact came back to bite him right in the proverbial ass.

***

I'm just too good at my job, Buck rationalized. *I need to cut back a little, maybe take a vacation again—nap for another 500 years...*

He had backed away from the unloading detainees as slowly and quietly as possible, and was now making his way down on the curved avenue, closer to the towers. Buck was doing his best to remain unseen, but as traffic increased, that was quickly becoming an impossibility.

He rounded the bend, and nearly ran into former Music Worlders tycoon Lars Mangros and his muscle, Yarat—two yutzes Buck had put away when they had tried to use subliminal messages to turn the galaxy's youth into a rampaging army. Somehow, they had gotten past him and were in the front now, coming his way. Lost in conversation, the two "detainees" hadn't noticed him yet. Turning to go back the way he came, Buck saw things were about to get much worse. Coming up behind him was a pack of goons led by M.D. Toman, a diminutive silver-haired man from the heavy gravity world of Lanseng XII. Toman had superhuman strength in Earth standard gravity; Buck shuddered to think how strong the little guy would be with his boots dialed down on Enceladus. Being that Toman was also likely holding a grudge against Buck, and the fact that he could bend steel with his bare hands, Rogers didn't want to head in his direction, either.

Luckily, just like Mangros, the tiny strong man hadn't noticed him yet. Trying to blend into the nearest wall, Buck pressed his back up against a tarp-covered permaslab barrier and swallowed.

"The mouse was right," he muttered out the side of his mouth. "It really is a small universe, after all."

With nowhere left to turn, Buck was trapped.

That's when the tarp came to life.

Thick-gloved arms stretched out from behind it, pulling Rogers off his feet and into the dark recesses within.

"Yulp!" was all he had time to say.

It wasn't his most eloquent soliloquy.

Behind the tarp, there was a cramped alley between permaslab blocks. Whoever had pulled him in had taken him out of harm's way.

Or had they?

With the stranger bodily hidden behind him, one of those heavy-gloved hands suddenly clamped over Buck's mouth, while the other held a shiv neatly at the base of his spine.

The indication was clear—keep quiet or you're dead. Buck complied.

For now.

Through an open sliver in the tarp, Buck watched the two groups of his former foes converge. They stopped and chatted for a bit. One of them told a joke that most of them found funny. Buck imagined they were talking about him, and how they'd like to spit him like a roast if they ever got their hands on him again. Finally, a guard came by to break them up and get them to their work stations.

As the detainees wandered off, his attacker's grip loosened, and soon the gloved hand dropped from Buck's mouth. Finally, the mysterious stranger spoke.

"I think that's three lives you owe me, Buck Rogers—but who's counting?"

He knew the voice. With one move, Buck disarmed his assailant and whirled around to face them. He pinned the not-so-stranger's arms as the now discarded shiv—an ice shard—twirled away lazily towards the ground in the low gravity.

It was a woman from his past—roughly a year ago.

She wasn't wearing the red catsuit with the cut-out thighs and bullet bra as when they first met. Instead she wore a detainee grade hot suit and engineering gloves that were four sizes too big for her. Where her hair was once long and curly, it was now straight and cut in a bob.

But there was no mistaking those sarcastic eyes, nor her cynical smile.

Letting go of her arms, he pinned her in a bear hug instead.

"Joella!" he exclaimed. "Am I glad to see you!"

ACT IV

Joella Cameron: one year ago.
She didn't know Buck from a hole in the wall, and had saved his life anyway. The terrorist group known as the Legion of Death had used her to identify Rafael Argus—an assassin coming to join their ranks, and one whom Buck was impersonating in order to infiltrate them. The Legion had a plot to kill a city—New Chicago, to be exact—and Buck was the only one standing in their way. Joella knew Rafael, but had never met Buck. Nethertheless, she had decided to play along, and had not turned Rogers in.

"Thanks," Buck offered, modestly.
"You're welcome, uh—"Joella struggled for something to call him.
"Buck Rogers," he smiled.

"You are taking an awfully big chance, Buck Rogers." Joella began to walk the room. *"Trying to fool Sherese and her friends, that's risky enough."* She turned towards him. *"But, uh, how do you know I won't blow your cover?"*

"You look like somebody I can trust," he told her.

"I just look like somebody you can trust?" Joella chuckled. *"Boy, you must get hurt an awful lot."*

"Sometimes you get hurt no matter what you do," he replied. *"You can't let that stop you trusting people."*

Joella laughed again. "Sure you can, after you hear the same old lines year after year," her words dripping with cynicism, *"asking you to trust and to care for as long as they need you."*

Buck could tell she had been hurt, probably many times.

Joella continued. "And then they leave you, and you're alone on some godforsaken planet, and you don't even know where home is anymore..." she trailed off, lost in an unpleasant memory. Then: *"Sure you can,"* she rallied, snapping back to the present.

"Joella, everybody gets hurt." Buck was never more serious. *"But everybody doesn't hurt everybody."*

She didn't want to, but Joella found herself believing him. It was in his eyes.

"I'll hold you to that, Buck Rogers."

***

Now on the moon of Enceladus, in the cramped alley of a forced labor mining camp, Buck Rogers was standing face to face with Joella again.

"I don't get it." Buck was at once delighted and confused to see her. While she had clearly saved his bacon—again—hwe couldn't fathom what she would be doing on the prison moon.

Joella, how'd you get yourself in trouble again?

"After we dealt with Kellogg and his goons, I got you set up in New Chicago. You had an apartment, the Directorate found you a job—"

"Yeah, tending bar," she interrupted. "It was thrilling. I found out I wasn't the only one you did that for, you know. I did my research, and..." she hesitated. From the look on her face, Buck guessed that she was unsure if she was willing to give up her informant.

She gave up her informant.

"Twiki told me everything. I found out about Tangy, and Stella, and—" Joella went on, one name after another.

Buck rolled his eyes. *Dammit Twiki.* Explaining context wasn't one of the ambuquad's strong points. *When I get back, there's a short circuit in your future...*

"What do you do—travel the galaxy, collecting women and setting them up in apartments around the Federation?"

He didn't have an answer for that. It was almost right, but he wouldn't call it "collecting." And it wasn't done for any ulterior motive. He was trying to help those in need, getting them set up for a new life, a new start.

All this is out of context, that's all, it's...

"A girl gets lonely waiting to be the one you visit, Buck," she spat. "So, one night, when a gun runner came in and made me a business proposition, I took him up on it." She threw her arms up in despair. "How was I supposed to know the whole thing was an undercover operation set up by the Security Directorate?"

"You could have called me," he admonished her, "I would have pulled some strings and gotten you out of it. I—"

"And be indebted to you again?" She was incredulous. "Sorry, Buck. Sometimes I want to be responsible for myself."

Defeated, Rogers sighed and sank down on an overturned storage crate, his back against one of the permaslab blocks. He looked truly hurt, something she wasn't expecting. Considering what he had just said, Joella tilted her head.

"...pulled some strings?"

When that didn't elicit a response, not even the usual, "forget it," she sat down next to him, touching his hand.

"Look, its not that I don't appreciate what you did for me, or tried to do, but... sometimes you've got to leave well enough alone, you know?"

Buck was quiet.

"You can't always go around saving everybody, Buck Rogers."

Buck stood up, his back to her. For a long moment, he remained silent.

Finally, he spoke. "No, Joella." He turned to look at her, more determined than ever. "That's exactly what I'm going to do—starting with these people right here," his eyes glanced around, "who all hate me."

"Then," he took a step closer to her, "I'm going to go save the Earth," he paused. "Again."

"Now," Buck reached out for Joella's hand, "will you help me?"

Joella stared at his hand for a second, before letting herself break out in a giant smile.

"Same old Buck Rogers," she laughed, shaking her head. "You'll never learn, will you?"

"Not in another 500 years," he smiled back.

After checking the coast was clear, they made their way towards the center of camp.

Hand in hand.

The camp was coming alive. Men and machinery hummed and bustled as payloads were sent down the mineshaft, workers retracted drills and lasers, and energy dampeners were set to prevent any explosions below from reaching the surface. Buck and Joella spiraled down the busy avenues, moving ever closer to the mine itself. Making sure he stuck to the shadows, Buck asked questions along the way.

"When the order came from Earth to harvest the microbacteria, the Warden decided against using drones for the dangerous work," Joella explained. "Instead he put the detainees to work."

"That makes no sense." He was more baffled than ever. "Why force the pris—the detainees—to do manual labor when a machine can do it faster and without risk?"

"Because it was a machine's idea," she countered.

"Maximus," Buck scowled.

The rehabilitation facility's warden is in cahoots with Maximus.

Joella nodded. "And, we were given a choice, at first. We were offered a reduced sentence if we did it. A few jumped at that, but not many. Those who didn't, we..." Joella was getting flustered.

"Hey." Buck pulled her aside and tried to soothe her.

"Hey, it's okay. I'm here, remember?" he smiled. "Whatever it is, it's the past; it can't hurt you anymore."

Joella slowly nodded again. "We were all given... special treatments," she said, closing her eyes, trying not to remember the details of her ordeal. "Maximus had some expert modify the O.E.I. scanner to cause pain. They would... *condition* us to do the work. Either we did it or we'd go back under the psych probe."

Buck put his hand on Joella's shoulder, encouraging her to continue.

"A few were still defiant, and were kept under the probe for days," she shuddered. "No one has seen them since—we don't even know what happened to them."

"Well, where's this warden?" Buck demanded. "Why is he kowtowing to Maximus's decrees?"

Joella was puzzled. "cow-how?"

Buck motioned quickly with his hand. "Come on!"

"You really don't know, do you?"

Now he was exasperated. "Know what?"

Joella sighed. "Maximus and the rest of the quads on this moon overthrew the rehabilitation center personnel."

Buck's eyes grew wide as Joella revealed what he had just figured out for himself.

"Maximus *is* the warden."

***

Wilma could see that Harris fancied himself a gambling man.

For the past forty minutes, he had been playing Buck's copy of *Hologram 10 and 11* with the ship's computer.

And losing.

Over and over.

Wilma, however, was thankful he was distracted; she was busy doing some gambling of her own.

Using a trick she had learned back in her academy days from Duke Danton, Wilma was gently cycling power up and down to one of the energy leads that serviced the same node as the tractor beam. While completely harmless, the computer should read it as a power fluctuation.

With any luck, it should sound an alarm any—

> WARNING. POWER FLUCTUATION
> JUNCTION 4-8, POWER NODE 3-7.
> POSSIBLE POWER LOSS TO TRACTOR BEAM
> RECOMMEND IMMEDIATE INSPECTION and SERVICE.

Captain Harris quit his game and jumped out of his seat, reaching for the tools he had stashed in the cockpit.

"Oh, what now?"

As he headed aft to check on the tractor beam equipment, he waved his hand back at Wilma.

"Just keep her steady, Dex, this shouldn't take long. Probably nothing. Flying garbage scow—"

Wilma watched him go. As soon as Harris's head was buried deep in the inner workings of the tractor beam assembly, she tapped her upper jaw, and the subcutaneous transmitter/receiver concealed there.

"Buck," she whispered. "Buck, can you hear me? Come in!"

If ever she needed Buck Rogers, now was the time.

***

Wilma had called him.

Unfortunately, that seemed to be the only good news.

Something was fishy in Denmark, and Buck could tell Wilma smelled it, too.

All the way from Enceladus.

Happy to be in contact again, Buck breathed a sigh of relief that their subcutaneous communicators worked as long as Wilma's shuttle was in under the forcefield. The two of them compared notes, bringing each other mostly up to speed. For various reasons, however, Buck decided not to mention Joella for the time being.

Neither Buck nor Wilma was very happy with the other's findings. Quickly, they began to hash out a strategy to improve the situation.

They had to secure the Archaea, and would need to put a stop to what Maximus was doing. Aside from just being wrong, using forced labor in the jurisdiction of the Terran system would not to be tolerated by the Science Council. First, however, Buck would need to get underground. He had to make sure that demolition den was actually safe before Wilma risked releasing a blazium warhead in it.

"If they haven't set it up right…" Wilma cautioned.

"I know, I know," Buck remembered how only a half a brick was enough to alter the course of a 10 billion ton spaceberg of frozen oxygen. But Buck wouldn't know if the den had been prepared or not by sight alone. He was going to have to get video.

"Once you upload the recordings to me, I'll have the computer analyze them and make sure it's safe. Otherwise, I'll have to commandeer this ship and steal the blazium from them."

Buck considered the implications and the resulting hammer that would come down hard on Wilma.

"Something tells me Maximus won't like that."

"He'd like it better than incinerating the entire moon," Wilma countered.

Succinct as always.

The two of them were just lucky that Wilma had been assigned the task of carrying the warhead. As old as their transport tug was, it seemed to be one of the best shuttles they had out here.

"Okay. So once we know both the blazium and Archaea are safe…" he paused.

For a while.

When the pause failed to give birth, Wilma interrupted.

"Buck?" she questioned. "You do have a plan for shutting the camp down, don't you?"

Buck again responded with silence.

"You always have a plan!" Wilma exclaimed.

This time, there was none.

***

Colonel Deering found Buck's lack of a plan disturbing.

Apparently, so did Buck.

"I don't know, Wilma." He actually sounded worried. "I'll try to hook up with Uma, and get her security force back in the loop, but even that'll give us a pretty small fighting force." He paused. "Under normal circumstances, I'd incite some kind of rebellion to overpower Maximus, his robo-goons, and their human henchmen. But from the looks of things, most of the workers here would want to kill me just as much as topple their overlords."

It occurred to Wilma just how right he was; Buck was too well known to the detention populace here. As soon as one of them identified Buck Rogers, the mob would be coming after him, not rallying behind him. Buck was in a very dangerous place, and was essentially exposed.

And they couldn't really count on the security team they had brought with them either—Wilma and Buck's cover stories were kept from them. As far as they knew, this operation was set up like this legally. Marshal Terrol might not even believe them. Wilma thought long and hard for a moment, finally deciding on a term from his century.

"Cavalry?" she offered.

Buck signed in agreement, "Cavalry."

They were in over their heads; calling for reinforcements from Earth was the only viable option.

"But how?" Buck was frustrated. "With that jammer in place..."

"I had a thought about that," she replied, punching up the computer diagram of the site and zeroing in on the three spires directly around the demolition pit. "I know I just asked you to go down to the demolition den, but do you think you can get to one of those crane towers afterwards?"

After another pause, Buck responded an affirmative. "Security is an issue, but it's not impossible."

Wilma smiled. *Of course not—not for you anyway.*

"In fact," Buck was up to something, "I think there's a way we can kill two birds with one stone."

Now she was completely lost.

"Birds?"

"Forget it," Buck sighed. "It means we can get both things done at the same time."

Unnecessary violence against avians aside, Buck's going to go 30 kilometers underground and *get to the 100 meter tall crane towers simultaneously?*

She didn't ask how. By now she knew better. Whatever he had in mind, it would work. It always did.

Usually.

Most of the time.

"What do you want me to do at those towers?" he inquired.

They needed to get word to Huer and Theo, and their only chance would be for Buck to disrupt the antenna array below, allowing Wilma to piggyback a message back to the directorate. She turned to see Harris still in the back, fine-tuning the tractor beam module. She'd have to talk Buck through this fast, and wouldn't get a second chance.

"OK," Wilma took a deep breath. "Listen carefully...."

***

Buck and Wilma weren't the only ones speaking in hushed tones. Standing at a workbench less than ten yards from Joella and Buck were five inmates on break, planning an escape.

The largest of them was Tamu, an immense fat man with dreadlocks. Nearly two meters tall with tanned skin, he used his immense bulk to hide their conversation from the guards standing in front of the mine entrance.

Another of the convicts, a limber blonde man named LeFeatt, was proposing a plan: hijack one of the transport shuttles carrying explosives, and use it to get off planet. The trick would be to use the explosives to make the security forces think the transport tug was destroyed, cut power, and continue on the proper vector until they reached a stargate.

With a little luck, they would be passed over as a meteorite until they drifted through the gate and could power back up on the other side of the known systems.

The shortest of them, Viril, spoke up first. As always, he was the "yes" man. "Yeah, yeah.. sounds good. I like it!"

Smarter, Tamu and LeFeatt turned to the eldest man present. His silver-white hair slicked back in a pompadour, Porter Sinclair silently considered the plan, mentally calculating food consumption, trajectory, and travel time to Stargate One.

Finally, as if noticing everyone was looking at him for the first time, Sinclair slowly nodded his head, and announced his conclusions.

"It could work."

"No," a raspy voice interrupted.

Barnes, usually the quiet member of the group, spoke for the first time.

"I have another plan," He croaked. "Better plan."

Clearing his throat, he stepped forward. His sunken features looking all the more ghostly in the pale fluorescence of the camp's energy fence. His voice less hoarse now, he continued.

"The demolition den. Blow up the blazium charge before it's in place. Blow up the detention center on Enceladus. Blow up Enceladus. End Earth's chance of fixing its problem. Kill everyone here with it."

They all knew that the den was packed with several charges that had been placed already, and more were being set now. The largest of the explosives—including the blazium—would be brought in to cap them off shortly.

Livid, LeFeatt grabbed Barnes by the collar.

"Now wait a minute, I'm not blowing myself to Neptune and back, here! My brother is still miss—" Tamu's giant hands came down like blast doors between LeFeatt and Barnes, cutting off his words and pushing them apart. Barnes just stared dead ahead, not into LeFeatt's eyes, but as if through the other man's head.

"Relax", the fat man grumbled softly in LeFeatt's ear, before turning to address the others.

"That's actually not a bad idea. We could use the threat to bargain our way out of here—they don't need to know how serious we are." The big man patted Barnes on the shoulder.

"That's what Barnes was talking about."

As the others nodded in agreement, Sinclair paid particular attention to Barnes.

His eyes were hollow voids.

The convict hadn't acknowledged anything Tamu had said; he simply continued to stare ahead as if into oblivion.

Part II

ACT I

"Got it. You, too." Buck tapped his jawline again, ending his conversation with Wilma. Multitasking as usual, he had been watching while listening, and had noticed the near scuffle between some of the inmates nearby. Grabbing Joella's attention, he motioned towards them now.

"Who are these bozos?"

Joella looked around the corner at the group by the workbench, pointing out the lithe man first. "That man over there? He is a convicted thief, Jean LeFeatt. He and his brother were caught smuggling Arzone off of Titan. His brother Rik fought the machines harder than Jean did—too hard. No one's seen him for weeks."

Buck nodded.

"The big guy's name is Tamu—I've had some trouble

with him." Buck waited for her to elaborate. "He's been chasing me around the compound since work started." Joella forced a smile. "Thinks he's my new boyfriend."

Buck smiled, "Not your type?"

"I think we both know my type." she retorted. "Tamu thinks he's smarter than he looks. He's actually been running guns for years without getting caught, but was finally arrested for starting a barroom brawl, of all things."

"Short fuse."

Remembering the 20th Century phrase, Joella agreed. "The little guy's name is Viril, he'll pretty much do whatever the others tell him to. He's in for minor league stuff. Creepy guy's name is Barnes, don't know much about him," she continued, "and the older man is Porter Sinclair. He's some kind of genius, and not a single one of us has any idea why he's here. Everyone assumes it must be something big, because his data is encrypted even for the Warden. Only the Security Directorate on Earth and Sinclair himself knows—and rumor is even Maximus' machines couldn't get it out of him."

Interesting little group, Buck pondered. *A thief, the muscle, and a henchman; the creep and the brains.*

Swinging her arms back and forth in anticipation, Joella brought him back to the task at hand. "So, are we going down to check out the demolition den, or what?"

Buck smiled again. "Well, about that…"

Joella stopped swinging. "I know that smile."

Sheepishly, Buck confessed. "I need you to go without me."

"What?"

"See, I can't join you—I've got a date with a comm antenna array." Now Buck had a plan. "But if you can get inside and get us some video of that demolitions den, Wilma can confirm that these yahoos aren't going to accidentally blow up the moon when they try to crack the crust here. Meanwhile, I can call in the cavalry and we can blow this pop stand."

She blinked twice before answering.

"Ya-whose?" she asked.

Buck opened his mouth to reply, but Joella was quicker.

"Pop-stand?" she added.

"Uh, forget it."

Unzipping his hot suit, Buck removed his belt, and slid the buckle off.

Amused, Joella watched.

"I thought you were a fast mover, but seriously."

Buck frowned. "Nice."

Buck and Wilma had brought along their own playthings, special gadgets supplied by Dr. Theopolis.

"Okay, look." Showing her the buckle, he forced himself to talk 25th Century. "Take this—its a communicator that takes pictures—uh—holograms. Record that demolition den for me. Upload it to Wilma so she can confirm the blazium she's carrying isn't going to accidentally incinerate all of us. You get into any trouble, you can use it to call me." Buck fought the urge to pace. "I'm going to override that jammer array and the Directorate will scramble forces to shut down this whole operation. Then I promise you we are all getting out of here. Do you think you can do that?"

Joella narrowed her eyes, as if she wasn't sure if she should trust him again.

Finally, she caved.

"Yeah," she rolled those eyes over. "I think I can handle it."

"Great." Buck handed her the device. "You know how to use one of these things?"

"Sure," Joella replied, slipping it into her hot suit. "Just point and click."

Buck smiled. *25th Century technology.*

"The only question is," Joella looked around before continuing, "how am I—or you—going to make it past the guards?"

Buck looked over at the four man team guarding the mine entrance, then at the guards watching the east tower, before finally settling his focus across the yard at the nearest maintenance pod. There were the same five detainees from before, still talking about escape—and still thinking no one noticed.

"Oh, I think I can whip up something," he offered, kissing her on the forehead.

And with that, Buck sauntered right into the group of detainees as if he belonged.

He most assuredly did not.

"Hey, guys!" Buck greeted them. "Whatcha up to?"

His bombastic appearance caused everyone present to shut up and recoil instantly. Buck put himself directly in the middle of their little circle, leaning against the recharge pole and crossing his arms.

"Oh, come on—don't be bashful. I thought I heard something about an escape plan," he teased. "What's so bad about the work here, anyway?" Buck dropped his eyes to Tamu's paunch, met his gaze, and smiled. "From the look of it, you guys could use the exercise."

As expected, Tamu boiled over first. "Mintie," he managed to grind out, "what's your name?"

Mintie? Buck thought about it for a second. *Mint, as in newly minted.*

"Oh, you mean like the new guy," Rogers smiled. "Got it!"

Buck stood tall and tried to meet Tamu's eyes. He came about as far as the fat man's chest. "Mateo," Buck offered, "Name's Anthony Mateo." Buck looked away, seemingly bored. "But you don't need to remember it," he pointed to his security patch on his own shoulder, before returning Tamu's stare once again. "You can just call me 'Sir.'"

"Mateo?" LeFeatt seemed confused. Tamu looked back the way Rogers had come, and saw Joella standing there, arms crossed and shaking her head. Tamu turned his attention back to Buck real quick. "Hey," the big guy accused, "you been talking to my girlfriend?"

Before Buck could reply, LeFeatt interrupted.

"No, wait—Mateo—that name ain't right." He took a step closer towards Buck. "I know you from somewhere."

Oops. Buck flashed that cheshire grin of his while his eyes bored into LeFeatt. "You must be mistaken."

His confidence brought LeFeatt down a notch. While a second ago the convict had seemed on the verge of identifying Buck, now he wasn't so sure. "Yeah?" Doubt crept into LeFeatt's voice.

"Yeah," Buck was adamant. "We don't run in the same circles. I'm a security guard," he paused for effect, "not a garbage man."

Even with all money on Tamu, LeFeatt took the first swing. Buck, of course, was still one step ahead of him, immediately dropping to the ground and sweeping his feet with enough force to dislodge LeFeatt's boots and send him flying. As Barnes reached for LeFeatt to keep him from flying off, Tamu's meaty hooks sank into Buck's shoulders, pulling him off the ground and easily flinging Rogers overhead in the near null gravity. Sinclair did nothing but step back, his hands clasped behind him.

As the spinning Buck flew towards the maintenance pod, he realized he was in trouble. He was going too fast and his trajectory was all wrong; he wasn't going to hit the pod, he was going to sail over it. With Enceladus's gravity so low, he might even land *outside the breathable zone.*

Just as he was about to clear the pod, Buck remembered something.

Something important.

Magnetic boots!

As his foot neared the maintenance pod, Buck cranked the dial to MAX. With a reverberating metallic 'clang', he stuck instantly to its side. He was hanging upside down, magnetically attached to the pod a meter and a half above the ground by one foot, but he was safe. Buck beamed.

"Must be my personality," he said.

"ARRRRRRRRRRRHHHHH!" was the only reply.

Captain Rogers looked up to see the freight train called Tamu barreling towards him, grasping for his throat.

Buck pulled himself close to the pod, tucking his limbs in like a cannonball. Dialing his boots to REPEL, he kicked off the metallic wall, barreling right into the oncoming Tamu.

The bullet formerly known as Buck Rogers smashed into Tamu hard, knocking the fat man out for the count.

As Buck struggled to disentangle himself from the unconscious behemoth, his cronies took the chance to start a riot. One of them hurled his tool case into the nearby energy fence, causing it to erupt in sparks. Every detainee in the yard who had witnessed the brawl let loose on one another, taking the opportunity to settle old scores.

Everyone except for Sinclair.

As the chaos ensued, the older man just stood there, assessing. Finally, the guards at the entrance to the deep mine stepped in, rushing forward and firing their pulse pistols on stun to suppress everyone. They were soon joined by the security watching the cranes.

Bingo.

The guard posts abandoned, Joella took the opportunity to dive into the mine. She paused once at the entrance before disappearing into its depths—just long enough to give Buck an enthusiastic "thumbs-up."

Buck returned the gesture and slipped away towards the crane towers.

Thumbs-up all around.

***

Garrett's security force might be easily distracted, but they knew their jobs, and did them well.

Within fifteen minutes, the rioters were rounded up, shackled, and corralled off. In magna-binders now, the groggy Tamu was forcibly sat down in the staging area next to the other troublemakers and pressed up against Sinclair, who had simply never moved. Soon Viril was seated nearby.

"Well, that was a fast shift," Tamu grimaced.

As the guards walked away, the large man spoke close-mouthed.

"That guard—Mateo—what the stars was that about?"

Sinclair made sure security was no longer paying attention before he replied. "He's watching us, is what it means. We'll have to be careful. I recommend we hold off any escape attempt until I can reassess the status quo."

Tamu shook his head affirmative.

"I have a feeling the, ah, new guard isn't as stupid as he looks," added Sinclair.

"Hey," Tamu nodded past the guards, "where'd he go?"

"Good question," Sinclair smiled, then observed, "and where's your *girlfriend?*"

As Tamu looked around for Joella, he noticed something else. "Where's Lefeatt and Barnes?"

Sinclair and Tamu exchange glances.

All four were gone.

***

One hundred thirty-four light years away, an Emperor lay dying.

Draco's health had deteriorated significantly over the past two years. To Ardala, it seemed as if he had never gotten over their defeat by the Terrans thanks to Buck Rogers's untimely intervention… an incident that was *partially* her fault.

Ardala admitted that much to no one but herself.

It was *Killer Kane* who had taken the brunt of the responsibility, and who had ultimately paid the price for her—their—*his* failure.

Ardala timidly stepped into her father's chambers, and was greeted by labored breathing. Before her, on an opulent floating platform bed, lay the immense bulk of Emperor Draco.

He had first become thin and frail, then lethargic and obese, so much so that now he was unable even to walk, and instead traversed the palace via hover platform. The doors to his quarters and his personal spacecraft had been widened, as had most of the doors on the command levels of all Star Fortresses—should he choose to travel the breadth of the Empire and lead his forces into combat. For the most part, however, he appeared as a hologram via the Empire's sophisticated holonet system, taking control of a ship in battle from the safety of far away, never having to face the immediate consequences of a tactical error, such as what led to the destruction of those Star Fortresses that went up against the Sauria or the Zykarians. For Draco, participating in battle had become not unlike a holographic combat simulation or, even what Buck had explained to Ardala as a "video game"—a primitive computer simulation game played by children and adults alike in the 20th century. The player was afforded a number of tries, or "lives," as Buck called them, to complete the game's assigned tasks. As one's scores increased, so did the number of lives. When the ship Draco commanded was destroyed, he simply transferred his hologram to another—another "life" to play.

His hover platform lay low to the floor, struggling to bear up under his tremendous weight. While covered in the finest cushions and silken sheets, they were soiled and unkempt.

Disgusting, Ardala noted with an involuntary grimace. *He's been shunning away his maid service again.*

On the bed itself were the remnants of last night's meal, a platter containing the half chewed leg bone of some large exotic animal, likely imported from one of the newest worlds that had been stomped beneath the heel of the Draconian warmachine. Never one to trust the running of that machine to others, Draco had a command console swung over the bed on an extension arm. From there he could control the large screen monitors throughout the room, and maintain a vise grip on his empire, health be damned.

Ardala noticed the newest additions to the bed—a phalanx of menacing medical equipment. Lighted tubes tracked photonic treatments directly to Draco's skin and the various organs beneath it, irradiating corrupt cells and nurturing the growth of good ones. To Ardala, the whole setup was more like some kind of torture rack than medical aid. His face in shadow, Ardala could not tell if Draco was awake or asleep. She gingerly addressed her father.

"Daddy? I bring news of the Terrans, I—"

"The Terrans," he coughed. "Yes, the Terrans. that is what I wish to speak to you about, daughter."

Close enough to see his eyes now, Ardala knew something was not right. They were sunken, withdrawn. Draco had always been larger than life, but now, despite his newfound immense size, the fire was out of him. For the first time in her life, Ardala was worried about her father.

"Daddy, are you alright?"

"The medtechs have confirmed it—I am nearing my last, daughter."

"Oh, Daddy, no!" Ardala threw herself over his mountainous body. It was this moment she had secretly hoped for and also feared most. She was the eldest daughter—the right of succession *was* hers. But her father could declare another more suited to rule—have her put to death, or even call for a *Conflict of Resolution*, which would pit her and her twenty nine siblings against one another in a war for dominance.

But Ardala knew she was her father's favorite—if not, she would surely be dead by now, for all her failures.

"It is not just me, my little princess…" Draco's words were drowned by a heavy wet cough. As he barked, the Emperor stabbed his fat finger at the command console, and the palace room itself shuddered. The sound of metallic clamps unlocking reverberated within the chamber, and there was a momentary sensation of downward motion before inertial dampeners in the sub-flooring kicked in. Draco had built his quarters into a safe room that could be lowered via a transport tube into the mountain itself. The entire Royal Suite steadily descended deep into the planet.

"It is the Empire as well," Draco wheezed. "All of the Draconian realm is dying."

***

The crane towers were enormous, and each one served a secondary function. From what Wilma had gleaned from the transport tug's new security computer, they worked in conjunction with a series of satellites in orbit around Saturn to serve as a communications jamming array, allowing only authorized transmissions to pass outside Enceladus's restricted zone.

If Buck could reset a few of one of the tower's relay circuits, they would be able to piggyback their own comm signals on any "official" transmission the camp sent out—and get word to Huer and Theo about exactly what was going on here.

He had found the panel Wilma wanted him to access, on a maintenance conduit half way up the thirty-story east tower. He had that panel open now, and was pushing colored pegs into a lighted board which bleeped each time he made an incorrect connection.

Red circuit transfer to J-10… or was it K?

"K!" he decided, plugging the red peg in.

The panel offered a dull flat tone as a reply.

Buck sighed. "You sank my battleship."

While he went over the connections Wilma had taught him again in his head, he could hear movement below. Buck froze, suddenly realizing that the sound was now coming from above. Something had moved passed him from within the crane's superstructure without noticing him.

That something was Jean LeFeatt.

Buck could read LeFeatt's IDent-number on the convict's back as he climbed—4200134. Apparently Buck and Joella weren't the only ones to take advantage of the confusion caused by the brawl. LeFeatt was up to something shady, something that was likely to not only get him killed, but to hurt a lot of people here, too.

Buck abandoned his sabotage for the moment and climbed after him, finally catching sight of the criminal on his knees at the top of the tower.

"LeFeatt!" Rogers called out from two stories below. "I just want to talk!"

***

Jean LeFeatt froze in his tracks at the sound of the guard's voice. It was that new security officer, "Mateo," that had followed him—he was sure of it. Now, LeFeatt would have to move fast. The shuttles had all delivered their payloads—twenty megatons of high density explosives. All that was needed now was the denotation cap. A single crust-buster composed of refined blazium—radiation free, it should just vaporize the super dense rock below the ice. As the others moved away, the last shuttle was coming in now to deliver that final payload.

Although positioned far from the crane towers, the last shuttle—an old style *Canarious* class transport tug—still flew as low as them to situate its deadly cargo. This was what LeFeatt had been counting on. He bent down to adjust the gravity setting on his magnetic boots.

The time was now.

***

"T minus 100 meters," Wilma reported. After Harris had given the tractor beam the go ahead, they finally got clearance to deliver their payload. The tug was essentially on autopilot; the security computer doing all calculations and flying. While she and "Andy" could essentially override the system and take control of the ship if necessary, it was best to leave the calculations to the machines at this point.

After all, she mused, *when was a computer ever wrong?*

Wilma smiled to herself. *Buck Rogers would not approve,* she thought. Having come from a time before everything was automated, Buck relied on his own instincts and skills to make calculations that would make the average 25th century man's head spin. While archaic, Wilma came to begrudgingly acknowledge those skills when he first demonstrated them, defeating the Draconian pirates who had beaten their combat computer systems with the help of rogue computer council member Dr. Apol, who had been reprogrammed as a traitor by Killer Kane himself before he defected to the Draconian Empire.

Wilma thought about that for a moment.

Despite Kane's influence, was Apol the start of what we have happening here? she pondered. Wilma knew Arin Kane more intimately than she would like to admit—and she of all people knew he was no master programmer. It's possible he didn't have to do too much modification to tap into the resentment the more advanced among these machines were already feeling towards mankind. Drones, ambu-quads, and computers had all been designed to do the work that was too dangerous for humans—yet here there was a reversal—the machines under Maximus were forcing humans to do the deadly work, in order to keep the risk to themselves minimal. Twiki and Dr. Theopolis had proven themselves not only invaluable coworkers, but friends time and time again. *Is it wrong to put machines capable of developing such bonds with sentient beings to work as menial labor?* She was beginning to question her own values. *Is that the same as slavery—or am I simply making the mistake of anthropomorphising robots because I've grown fond of two of them?*

"Deploying payload via tractor beam," Harris proclaimed, disrupting her reverie with a flick of a switch on his console.

Below the shuttle, a brilliant green cone of light hummed into place, gently lowering the tactical warhead down the cavernous ice tunnel that the detainees had been drilling with mining lasers, heat, and sound waves for over a month now. With precision and a little luck, they should have the well to the lower ocean finally blasted through and be able to start harvesting the bacteria they needed to keep the Earth on course to recovery. Then they'd be able to shut down this operation and get this whole human work force problem settled.

What could go wrong? she told herself.

Wilma sighed heavily.

***

Seeing the transport tug nearly level with the crane tower, Buck suddenly realized exactly what LeFeatt was up too. Wrongfully put to work or not, he couldn't let a convicted thief anywhere near a starship that was carrying explosives. Rogers popped his holster's clasp and pulled his blaster, taking aim at the crouching convict.

"LeFeatt—stop!"

But the criminal was already running.

As Jean LeFeatt took a running leap off the crane tower, Buck squeezed the trigger. The blaster bolt was close—singing LeFeatt's shirt. His jump was amplified by Enceladus's low gravity—less than zero point four-oh percent of Earth's.

And what a leap it was.

After sailing through the air for over 300ft, LeFeatt landed on top of the tug, rolling awkwardly to a stop—and in the process putting out the fire on the back of his hot suit. The rest of Buck's blasts went wild; LeFeatt was simply too far away for the limited range of the blaster to get off a clean shot at him.

Never taking his eyes off the situation at hand, Buck holstered his pistol and whipped out his assigned security comlink, depressing the stub that set off the detainee escape alarm. As the camp's lighting switched once again to a dull red hue and klaxons sounded below, Buck's eyes were looking to the heavens, searching that transport tug for an ID number, and finding one all too familiar.

GAL 0347...

...that's our ship.

That's Wilma.

That's not just some explosives—that cargo's the blazium warhead.

Rogers' paused on the tower's stairs, fiddling until he selected the correct channel on his comlink. "GAL 0347, this is Ground Security."

***

There was a muffled bump somewhere on the hull. Wilma quickly checked the scanner, but they were not in close proximity to anything nor anyone. Suddenly the detention center escape alarm sounded again, followed by a comm signal from Ground Security.

"Convict, uh... 42001—whatever, look—Jean LeFeatt—a detainee is piggy-backing your dorsal! Recommend you climb to a safe distance and await a security isolation team to subdue."

It was Buck!

Hearing his voice, Wilma moved to respond—but Harris beat her to the punch, pulling his comlink first. He depressed the talk stub, but paused and slowly turned to Wilma before responding.

"Piggy-back?" he inquired.

"I—" Wilma started, before realizing she didn't know, either. She smiled half-heartedly and shrugged her shoulders.

The man-boy was really annoyed now.

***

"Yes, piggy-back!" Buck yelled. "On your twenty! He—" Captain Rogers took a second to compose himself—and spoke in simpler terms. "He's right on top of your ship!"

"Thank you, Ground Security—this is Captain Harris. I'll get him off of us."

Watching LeFeatt position himself on board the shuttle, Buck tried to be polite to the Captain. "Uh, Captain, no offense, but LeFeatt is dangerous. He—"

"I'll handle it on my own," Harris snapped back, "thank you very much."

Why was it that bravado had beaten out common sense in the 25th century? Buck had had enough. "Harris! Listen to me, don't let him goad you into giving him what he wants."

Buck was insistent. "Do *not* open that airlock, capiche?"

***

"'Capiche'?" *Did he just insult me?* Captain Andy Harris was incredulous.

What in the solar system was a "capiche"? And who did this guard think he was—giving me orders—anyway?

He checked his comlink before slipping it into his belt, making note of the audacious guard's operating number. "Guard 033079—Officer Mateo, is it? Well, Officer, get off this frequency before I bust you down to cleaning detail!"

He turned towards Wilma. "Hold her steady," Harris ordered, strapping on his utility harness. Its accoutrements included both a blaster and a remote-control keyed directly into the *Canarious's* newly installed systems. By simply pressing the remote's dead-man's trigger, a panic signal would activate, and the craft would be unable to be flown anywhere without a retina scan from her commanding officer—or an officer of equal or greater rank.

As Harris bolted for the airlock, Wilma called out to him. "Maybe he's right, Harri—uh, Andy. We should—"

"You too? That's it. Consider yourself on report, Dex—both you and this Mateo person." Harris pointed his remote at the controls and fired. All the monitor screens on board GAL 0347 turned red, and the tug immediately went into hover-standby mode.

The cockpit controls were now useless.

***

Harris's comm signal went dead.

"Damn it!" Buck threw his comlink to the platform below him, where it lazily bounced before rebounding upwards again. He took up the stairs in leaps and bounds now, all the while stabbing at the subcutaneous transmitter located under his right ear.

"Wilma, get that ship away from the tower, now!" Buck demanded. "Do not let Harris open that airlock!"

***

In the *Canarious's* cockpit, Wilma unbuckled her flight harness, scrambling to go after Harris. "It's too late, Buck," she replied, tapping her upper jaw, "he's frozen the controls!"

In the cabin beyond, Harris pulled his blaster and thumbed the power setting to kill before cycling open the outer hatch. As soon as the door opened, LeFeatt's legs swung into the cabin, wrapped around Harris's neck, and pulled the startled man from the transport tug with a whoosh.

***

Holding onto a exterior grip above the now open egress-hatch with one hand, LeFeatt spun himself around so that Harris, while still choked between the convict's legs, was facing him. His legs were like a vice around the Captain's crushed throat, leaving Andy not much time to consider anything else.

After a single dazing punch to the face, LeFeatt took the man-boy's blaster. He then pulled the remote from his utility harness and pointed the device at the Captain's one open eye. Reading his retina, the buttons on the remote turned from red to green.

With that, LeFeatt smiled, released Harris, and simply punted the dazed man away.

***

Buck was approaching the top of the crane now, just in time to see the unconscious Harris catapulted from the transport tug and soar overhead across the Saturn filled sky.

"Huh," he muttered to himself. "Kickoff looks good—we just might even get a touchdown."

He stared at the airborne man's trajectory for a moment more. "Either that or make orbit."

At this low gravity, it would take Harris some time to reach the surface, and it was more than likely he would survive, landing within the atmospheric force field's range. For all intents and purposes, however, the imbecile was out for the count.

Buck shook his head.

"Yeesh."

***

As Wilma stood up from the co-pilot's seat, the monitor screens switched from pulsing red to displaying normal ship's functions—the *Canarious's* controls were back online. She hesitated for only an instant before whirling around to face LeFeatt. The convict held Harris's blaster in one hand, the remote in another. Before she could act, he spoke, simply, and to the point.

"Don't," he said.

His tone was flat and cold.

Wilma quickly glanced at the weapon pointed at her, noting it was set for kill. Her eyes darted upward, meeting her assailant's gaze. His eyes were not those of a desperate man, but of someone with nothing left to lose.

No doubt, LeFeatt was indeed dangerous.

"Hands up. Slowly," He added, motioning to the still open airlock. "Now, get off this ship or die."

"Alright," Wilma said, smiling cautiously as she raised her arms above her head. As she pushed her seat away from the control console, however, she kicked the starboard thruster array stub hard, sending the transport tug careening to the right—and barreling straight for the crane tower itself.

LeFeatt sailed right past her, bashing his head on the viewport, his blaster smacking Wilma in her face before flying across the cockpit to parts unknown.

***

Outside, another kind of smackdown was threatening to take place.

As the side of the ship rushed up to greet him, Buck's eyes widened with fear.

"Whoa, boy!" he stammered, before hurling himself from the tower's platform *directly towards the oncoming vehicle!*

ACT II

"Oh, Daddy, don't be so melodramatic." It was just like her father to think the Empire couldn't survive without him. The dynasty would continue; the legacy would endure. The realm would not die with the loss of its Emperor.

One thing would change, of course, Ardala rationalized. *The Empire will be mine.*

In the heart of the Draconian Empire, deep within Mt. Draconis, the royal chambers continued to descend, and a dying Emperor confided in his eldest Princess.

"It's true," he sputtered. "The war with the Saurians does not go well, daughter."

Draco punched up a code on his command console, and a tactical map sprang to life on the nearest wall's largest monitor. The map showed the Empire, but there were large blinking sections highlighted in red—all nearest to Sauria.

Maps bored Ardala. "Daddy—"

"Focus!" he commanded.

As she moved to the wall to humor her father, Draco continued.

"We have lost five sectors to the reptilian devils—and with it, our food colonies. Over resourced, our planets can no longer sustain their populations." He pressed another button on his console, and the map was replaced by a pictograph on a steady downward curve. Ardala didn't need her father to explain that it was not representative of good news.

"Without the food colonies—" she started.

"—the Empire has a maximum of twelve years left before it starves," he confirmed.

Draco leaned close to his daughter—a move that took great effort for him to accomplish in the first place, and then even more for him to stop himself from catapulting over the side of the hover platform. The device creaked and strained beneath his bulk.

"Do you see, Ardala?" He was insistent. "We must invade to survive! We must expand!"

Ardala saw it all too well—and saw another cause for alarm. *If this information became known...*

"Daddy, who knows about these numbers?"

"No one, save myself," Draco heaved, "and the Grand Vizier. All other commanders have either fallen in combat or were put to death."

"And, of course," he added, "now you know, as well, my dear." Draco cracked a broken smile, his teeth yellowed and brown.

"Enemies, both within and without the realm, would use this to their advantage." He removed a data stick from his computer, and motioned for Ardala to take it.

"Guard this data well, Ardala. You may share the information with Commander Kane—no one else."

Ardala snatched the stick from her father. "Absolutely no one else," she agreed.

With a hearty clang, the mobile royal chambers came to an abrupt stop.

"Ah!" Draco exclaimed, pressing yet another button on his console. The doors to his quarters opened wide to reveal blackness. He directed his floating bed through those doors, disappearing into the pitch beyond. Ardala stood where she was, impatient. Draco's voice beckoned her from beyond, echoing in the darkness.

"Come on, then! Indulge an old man's eccentricities but one last time, Ardala dear. Follow me."

Ardala sighed heavily, then followed.

***

Buck loved to ride the vomit comet.

Let me explain.

While training for space missions with NASA in the 1980s, the "vomit comet" was a nickname given to an aircraft that was used to give its occupants the sensation of weightlessness. By following a parabolic elliptical course, relative to the Earth's core, the ride would induce the sensation of freefall at a certain point in the plane's flight path. For 20th century Earth, it was the closest thing that man had technology-wise to approximate the zero gravity of outerspace.

Statistically, about a third of the personnel riding an aircraft performing this parabolic maneuver would become violently ill, another third would be moderately sick, and the final third would be unaffected at all.

NASA's definition of "ill", in most cases meant projectile vomiting—- hence the nickname, the vomit comet.

By 1986, Captain Rogers had personally logged several hours on the plane, never once becoming "ill." He was able to perform acute maneuvers during those periods of weightlessness, performing in the 90th percentile. In the end, he was evaluated as a well suited candidate for "prolonged periods of weightlessness in outer space, as well as the severe shifts in gravity caused by variable g-forces."

It was that acute maneuver training that Buck was dusting off for use right now.

As the side of the fifty-ton transport tug barreled towards him and the crane tower assembly, Buck quickly dialed his boots down to zero and kicked off the tower directly at the metallic behemoth.

Now in a deadly collision course of his own making, he tucked in his limbs and head and said a silent prayer that he had "eye-balled" his trajectory right. It was a calculated risk with enormous repercussions, but the only one to come to mind in the literal two seconds he had to "do or die."

Besides, after all—he was Buck Rogers.

***

Just before the ship plowed through the crane tower, Buck cannonballed directly into the still open airlock of the transport tug, rolling to the *Canarious's* deck within as her "normal gravity" interior took hold of him. In the next instant the tug sheared the crane in half, its metallic superstructure gift-wrapping around the mid-sized starcraft like a ribbon wrapped around a box of unwanted socks under a Christmas tree.

"A hole in one, and just a little off the top," Buck said to no one in particular.

The ship violently listed back away from the tower. Buck realized that in the demolition den below, the tractor beam cushioned warhead must had collided with the wall of the pit. Like a counter weight, the crash caused the shuttle up above to snap back into position, taking the twisted wreckage of the crane with it.

As the ship finally stopped shaking from the collision, Buck used his momentum to roll directly to his feet, quickly surveying the situation.

Like the airlock, the door to the cockpit was also still open. Within, Wilma was struggling to get the rabid LeFeatt off of her; his hands coiled thickly around her throat. A blaster lay in the connecting corridor; lost in the scuffle to regain control of the shuttle. As of yet unnoticed, Buck rushed the cockpit, just as Wilma's fist smashed directly into LeFeatt's already bloodied face.

The force of her blow threw the bewildered convict directly at Buck, his head clocking into Buck's in a mid air collision. The two collapsed in the doorway as a tangled sprawling mess. The confused Rogers pushed the dazed LeFeatt off of him; the criminal ultimately sliding down the cockpit controls as he slipped into unconsciousness.

"Ow," Buck said, picking himself up off the deck.

Either Wilma's got one hell of a right hook—or LeFeatt's head is full of bricks.

He shook his head to get rid of the circling stars.

Or both.

"B-Buck?" Wilma stuttered, getting her wind back. "How did you—"

"I was in the neighborhood," Rogers shrugged, flashing that lopsided grin of his. "I just thought I'd drop in."

***

In the labor camp below, there was orderly chaos.

As soon as a detainee escape attempt alert has been transmitted, the camp had gone into lockdown. Riot control protocols designed to keep the detainee population in check were activated—and the security teams finally began herding all convicts into their transport pods.

The man called Porter Sinclair had watched it all from the same work bench Mateo—and that was not the guard's real name—had last seen him at. A mathematical genius, Sinclair had already calculated Jean LeFeatt was behind this particular escape attempt. He calculated that it would fail, and made no move to be a part of it—even after LeFeatt had used the scrap with the guards to slip away. He had even noticed the girl, Joella, had been talking to Mateo before the fight had broken out, and that she had slipped past the guards into the deep mine.

She and the man calling himself Mateo were working together, somehow.

There was very little Sinclair didn't see.

Now finally being ushered into a detainee transport pod by the guards, the old man was contemplating the odds once again, and found them disturbing.

Barnes had yet to play his hand.

***

Time was not on her side.

It had taken Joella much longer to get down to the demolitions den than she had hoped. Someone had followed her in as she had entered the mine, and she had been forced to hide as the stranger had commandeered the high speed elevator to the lower levels. By the time it returned, so had security, and she had to wait for the right moment—a second alarm that she could only guess Buck must had set off—to finally descend. Finally here, the first thing she noticed were the security guards—all lying about with blast marks on their chests—all dead.

Whoever had beaten her down here was up to no good of their own. With haste, Joella moved from the outer support corridors cut from the ice and towards the rocky core chamber itself.

The den was tremendous.

This equatorial region of Enceladus was unlike the polar caps. Here there was none of the friction caused by tidal stresses, no warming of the underside of the ice sheet by overactive tectonic plates pulled back and forth by an overzealous Saturn. Instead, the entire surface was frozen through—there was no sea directly beneath a layer of ice. The only place on the moon where the Archaea lived, however was here—in subterranean oceans, beneath the planet's mantle, beneath kilometers of dense rock. It was from the topmost layer of that rock that the demolitions den was hewn.

About a kilometer tall, the carved out chamber curved inward along both the floor and ceiling like a flattened sphere. At its bottom were layer upon layer of explosive loads surrounded by catwalks, glowing power feeds and machinery of various kinds. These conventional bombs were packed into shaped charges designed to force their efforts downward and through the mantle, towards the life-giving sea below.

Joella quietly slipped onto the nearest catwalk, moving stealthily towards the center of the chamber and recording everything as she went. Above her, directly in the center of the distant ceiling was the yawning maw of the tunnel to the surface, some thirty kilometers away. Descending from that maw was the blazium warhead, wrapped in the protective green field of a tractorbeam. Icy debris fell from the tunnel's walls and peppered the explosive packages below. Joella could tell the warhead had collided with the sides of the mineshaft: whoever was piloting that tug must be a real vape-head.

As she moved, she took care not to tread on any bodies; there were quite a few more dead to be found here than in the service areas, all fresh kills, the acrid smell of ozone and burnt flesh evidence of their recent passing. Careful not to make a sound, Joella activated Buck's holographer again and began recording the demolition den. Suddenly, the picture went dark—something was blocking the recorder's viewport.

Someone was standing in front of the recorder.

Not someone—something.

Joella looked up and into a nightmare.

A ghoulish face stared back at her, its sunken eyes vacant, dead. The former man reached for her and stumbled, its gait broken and awkward. Its mouth opened as if to say something, but no intelligible sound issued forth. Instead, only a low moan escaped its cracked, weathered lips.

Startled, Joella gasped and leapt back, immediately smacking into something solid. She whirled, only to find she had stumbled right into another of the creatures. Everywhere she turned there was another; she was surrounded.

Before she had a chance to scream, they descended on her.

***

All around Ardala was nothingness.

The cavern into which she and King Draco had exited the royal chambers was black as pitch, and her father had either rounded an unseen corner somewhere, moving out of sight, or he had turned off his hover platform's ambient illumination in order to toy with her.

"Daddy?" Her voice reverberated far away, slowly coming back to her in waves. She had once been lost in Mt. Draconis's lava chutes as a child, having been lured there by her younger sisters in one of their bids to be rid of her. Alone, in the dark, Ardala had learned on her own then that echoes could twell you something about the size of the cavern you were in. The ringing of her voice was telling her now that wherever she was, it was immense indeed.

Exasperated, Ardala had finally had enough.

"Daddy!" she put her hands on her hips, defiant, her voice echoing all around them. "Really."

With a flair for the dramatic, the invisible Draco pounced on another control. "Let there be light!"

As sunstones blazed to life far above them, Ardala realized they must be deep within the planet. This prodigious cavern was tens of kilometers in diameter: Star fortress class ships like the *Draconia* hung in anti-gravity fields far above, amidst a latticework of gantries and enormous mechanical clamps, all in various stages of construction. Squadrons of Draconian Marauders—their latest fighters—hung from the ceiling, nose down like magma-bats, ready for the auto conveyors to move them into position at any number of former lava passages now converted to launch tubes.

It was here, deep beneath the surface, that the rich mines and veins of radioactive ore of Gamma Draconis III built the Draconian war machine.

All the star systems wondered why Draco had forged his empire from this inhospitable rock. But what Draco knew was that while there were certainly more pleasant worlds in the

Empire, none was as rich in the resources necessary for the war effort. No one save the Emperor, his most trusted advisors, and the men, women, and slaves who worked, lived and died here knew of its location. This was the Empire's womb, where all her warships were birthed. Her enemies could try as they might, but they would never find Draconia's secret shipyards, because they were *inside the planet itself.*

Ardala knew of this place, of course, being of royal heritage. Her father had even brought her here once before, when the *Rastaban* was rechristened. This time, however, something was different. Something had changed.

Above them suspended within the monstrous cavern, was an equally monstrous weapon.

The thing pulsed with a heartbeat of its own.

Its mammoth energy coils were as thick around as her space yacht, and looked to be nearly as long as the *Draconia* herself. Its general shape was that of a hexagonal cylinder, its maw honeycombed with an intricate substructure of webbing and lattice-like layers. Its support arms were connected to a gridworked drydock, photon umbilicals feeding it power converted from the very geothermal energies of Mt. Draconis itself. Ardala imagined that in use, the weapon would be mounted to the underbelly of a Star Fortress—the power connections hooking directly into the ship's massive contratureen engines.

The gargantuan behemoth above them continued to power up. Its skin seemed to glow from within, its heartbeat-like rhythm quickening emitting a familiar tune in a somewhat different key. The cavern resonated with a deep rumbling version of the whirring howl the alien pyramid weapon had made when Ardala attempted to... *persuade* Buck into wedded bliss with her.

The pyramid weapon that Buck had destroyed.

"The scientists call it a mass collector," Draco shouted. "The plans for it were in the databanks of the Annisud device the exploration corps brought back from their little trip to the galactic center."

Draco's look said his unspoken words.

The pyramid weapon she had lost.

Ardala rolled her eyes. Draco moved on, marvelling at his new toy.

"We of course had to build this one ourselves. The first round of scientists involved told me it couldn't be done," Draco sniffled, "that our technology was not as advanced as the aliens who designed it."

Insolence. Ardala knew what Draco would say next.

"I had them executed." He turned to her, his face a feverish grin. "The second science group seems to have done just fine," he nodded gleefully. "Just fine."

***

The undead horde closed in on her from all sides.

Joella slammed her eyes shut and covered her head, resigned to her fate.

When nothing happened, she opened one eye. One zombie was vapidly touching her hair. The dozen others were packed around her, standing there distracted and confused. While yes, they were way too close for polite conversation, they were in no way attacking her. They weren't even threatening.

They were just...

...sad.

It was then she began to recognize some of them, too.

Willis Alvar. Tem Emon. Even Rik LeFeatt—Jean's brother.

They were the troublemakers when Maximus had taken over, the ones who refused to play by his new rules. They were the detainees who fought back too hard.

"Rik?" She shook the creature she used to know from the rehabilitation center.

"Rik, do you understand me?"

His response was to emit an insipidly long string of drool from his half open mouth. The vacant-eyed Rik barely acknowledged her direction, let alone her words, looking more through her than at her.

The saliva strand stretched, nearly touched the floor itself.

They weren't "undead," but they might as well be. Maximus's machines had broken their minds. Some had radiation burns, bleeding ears, and other ailments as well—the tell-tale marks of working in hazardous conditions not meant for organic life. It was then that Joella realized there wasn't a single robot, quad or android down here. These men *were* the drones doing the dangerous labor. With the guards and other staff dead, they had no masters, and were wandering around aimlessly, milling about like a city of the dead.

But who bothered to kill the ones in charge, yet leave these poor creatures alive? Joella pondered. *A murderer who has pity?*

Then she noticed him.

There was someone else here, but he was unlike the others. While the mind-drained detainees shuffled about, this man instead was working methodically at the base of the explosives pit.

Joella had found her mysterious stranger.

He stood over the mining charges, connecting photon conduits to various machinery with apparent pride in his work. Recognizing him, she used the comm unit's holographer to try to get a better record of his face for whomever would be watching this lightshow, and then focused on the explosives and detonators.

Someone else had to know what was going on down here.

Come on, Buck...

***

Buck Rogers had just finished magna-cuffing Jean LeFeatt to the ship's recycler when Wilma called him back to the cockpit.

"What is it, Wilma?" He was in a good mood, despite having been nearly crushed by the transport tug and clocked in the face with LeFeatt's head. "And please don't tell me we've got a gremlin sitting on the wing."

Not getting the reference, Wilma nonetheless pressed on. "My belt buckle is flashing."

"Well, Wilma, everyone's gotta start somewhere." Buck winked at her. She scowled at his joke.

"It means I'm getting an upload signal." Wilma studied the pattern of binary strobes coming from her belt. "It's... it's from your holographic communicator. Did you leave it somewhere, or are you accidently sending me a recording of the inside of your hot suit?"

"Joella!" Buck exclaimed.

"Joella?" Wilma asked. "You mean *Joella*, Joella? Aldebaran II, the Legion of Death, Joella?"

"Yes, Joella Cameron—that Joella," Buck added. "It's a long story."

When Wilma wouldn't stop waiting for an answer, he gave her one.

The condensed version.

Afterwards, Wilma frowned and shook her head at him. Disapprovingly.

Buck gave her his best puppy dog eyes."What?"

Wilma slipped open her belt buckle and plugged her own holographic comm unit into the ship's computer. On one of the central monitors, a fully interactive view of the demolition den below resolved.

Blurry and pixelated due to being shot thirty kilometers down on a limited range device, the picture regardless seemed to suggest that the warhead was held firmly by the tractor beam.

"Thatta girl, Joella," Buck encouraged the transmission. "Lets see what the set-up down there looks like."

The next thing in focus, however, was unexpected to say the least.

"Waitaminute..." Buck squinted at the low resolution holography.

"What... is that a *body*?"

It was the first of many.

There were several people—either unconscious or dead—lying on the ground. The upload jumped with static. There were several seconds of confusing movement and blurry shapes, before the image refocused on a single man working in the den below.

"Who's that…?" Wilma asked, punching a code into the computer. The image froze on the man's face.

"Barnes—another one of the con—detainees. One of the more creepy ones." Buck was growing concerned.

"Can we talk to Jo?"

Wilma checked her console. "No, it looks like she's got the comm unit switched off. I'll try signaling her."

As the video started again, Buck could see photon conduits behind Barnes, connecting to a makeshift hub with a pattern of lights that were ticking down in binary.

"Wilma, is that…"

"Looks like he's set up some kind of timer. A bunch of them, actually."

Buck tried real hard to make out the words written on the smashed glass case on the nearby wall. "Manual…"

Manual detonation controls.

Suddenly the channel went dead.

If the blazium is down there when the other explosives go off, and not positioned correctly...

"Wilma… I think you'd better retract that warhead."

ACT III

Barnes was on Joella before she even saw him move, pinning her wrist. Her grasp on it tenuous at best, the comm unit had scattered to the chamber's floor, its outer casing smashing across the rocky surface.

He leered at her.

Uh-uh," he taunted, making a sweeping motion towards the catatonic deep workers with his free arm.

"You saw the others? That's what's in store for all of us." He aped sincerity. "Not me, though, and now, not you. Not anyone! There's an easy way to end this," he insisted. "Come, look!"

Barnes dragged her closer to each of the detonators—leading her around the chamber and showing her his handiwork. "Each explosive's connected to its own timer. Instead of one bomb to stop, why not ten? Why not twenty-three?"

His smile beamed. "Can't stop them all—too late for that." Without warning, he released her wrist, spinning Joella loose and causing her to fall to her knees. Spreading his arms wide, Barnes positioned himself in the center of the cavernous demolition den, directly underneath the unearthly green warhead. He sighed, heavily.

"Just too late."

***

Wilma was fighting with the tractor beam—and losing.

First, she had scanned the holographic recording Joella had sent them and was rewarded with a green light on her instrument console. Their blazium payload looked intact—dented and scraped, but securely held within the confines of the tractor beam. Then the light next to the green one started blinking red.

"The tractor beam is not responding," Wilma declared. "The emitter is damaged!"

Wilma's hands were a flurry of motion over the controls, but to no effect. "Buck, I—I can't retract the warhead. The beam is holding the payload tight, but all I can do is leave it on or turn it off!"

And that would drop the blazium cap right into the demolition den. Without being precisely placed, when Barnes set off those explosives the blast would at best vaporize half the ice shelf—taking the labor camp and rehabilitation center with it—and at worst incinerate the entire moon. The other explosives already in the den didn't have the impact to take out much except collapse the tunnel without the direction of the shaped charge warhead.

Buck jumped into the other pilot seat, pulling the second set of controls to him.

"Then we climb!" he declared. "You just keep that tractor beam running, Wilma. Lets see how fast this crate can fly with a crane tied around it!"

Wilma nodded—their only chance now was to get the the warhead out of the pit and as far away from the coming blast as possible. And if they weren't high enough when the other explosives went off, the burst might just trigger their payload, and take Buck, Wilma, and the labor camp with it.

She flicked on the emergency transmitter.

"Attention all shuttles and personnel transports, evacuate the labor camp immediately," she demanded. "All security crews get the labor force to safety. Code Red! Code Red! explosion in the pit imminent!"

"Hold on to your hats," Buck said pulling back on the yoke.

Wilma knew that one; he'd said it before.

She had no hat.

She held on anyway.

***

Joella began to back away, slowly getting to her feet.

"Too late!" Barnes laughed now, basking in the tractor beam's eerie glow. Suddenly that light began to fade, the hum of the beam diminishing in kind. They both looked up; whoever had been keeping that warhead in place was now pulling it out of the demolition den, and up the ice shaft. From the looks of it, it wasn't moving all that fast, but it was going. Emergency alarms began to trill, echoing throughout the cavern.

There may be time, Joella thought.

"No..." Barnes whispered to the receding warhead. "NO!" he raged. "Come back!"

Joella noticed a red light beaconing in the corner darkness. She reached down, grabbed the broken holographer, and ran.

***

Buck and Wilma were moving, but not fast enough.

With the crane wreckage twisted around its hull, the transport tug flew like a brick. Buck pulled a circuit board from a wall panel, disabling a cut-off regulator with a spark. He then cranked the shuttle's antigravity thrusters past their safety limit, and the cumbersome ship shot straight up through Enceladus's barely existent atmosphere. As long as the warhead was within the demolition shaft, Buck couldn't engage the ship's main propulsion units. They had to clear the payload from the confines of the ice tunnel before changing orientation and blasting out of there.

"Come on, come on!" he growled.

***

Joella moved with purpose.

Vape-head or not, whoever was flying that shuttle was attempting to prevent annihilation. Without the blazium added to the mix, the camp just might survive, but the deep workers down here—the mind-wiped—didn't stand a chance, unless she could get them all into an emergency blast chamber.

She located one such compartment, and punched the emergency alarm. There was a click and a hiss, and the chamber's vault-like shield door began to open slowly.

"Come on," she started corralling the mindless men towards the still-opening emergency blast door. "Come on, we're all going now." She couldn't do this all by herself. There was no way she could stop Barnes in time, but she just might be able to save these men.

Joella needed help, and she knew it.

That's when she remembered the holographer Buck had given her was also a commlink. Pulling it out of her pocket, she noticed the red light on its side continued to blink lazily.

Was that an incoming call?

She hoped its cracked face didn't mean it would no longer function. She opened the channel and spoke.

"Hello? Buck?"

There was nothing.

This far down, no communicator would work—unless she had line of sight with the surface. Telling the deep workers to stay in the shelter, she ran back towards the demolition den, and the open shaft above.

***

The hammer-faced *Canarious* transport spiraled upward toward Saturn.

Buck attempted to compensate for the spin, but the transport tug's limited reaction control thrusters couldn't handle the additional load of the off-center mass wrapped around her.

Beside him, Wilma clutched the console, focusing on her controls instead of the stars spinning by the viewport. Killing the cut-off regulator had also disengaged the inertial dampeners and internal artificial gravity, meaning they were feeling the effects of their deadly gamble.

They were down to the last kilometer of tunnel.

"1000 meters… 750…" Colonel Deering counted down.

"We'll make it, Wilma."

There's not enough time…

"700… 650… Buck…"

"Wilma," he spat, "I'm not dropping that bomb on these people!"

"Neither am I." Wilma set her jaw and stared ahead, defiant.

Buck felt like an ass. "I'm sorry, Wilma. I know you weren't saying that, I—"

Suddenly, his subcutaneous transmitter crackled to life.

"Buck?"

Joella?

"Joella!" Buck exclaimed, motioning Wilma to check her transmitter. She nodded; she could hear it as well.

"Where are you?" Buck was concerned.

Hopefully she's clear—

"I'm in the demolition den, Buck," Joella's voice trembled. "The 'drones' doing the dangerous work, they aren't robots at all, Buck. They're detainees whose minds have been broken!"

Joella sounded panicked. "Their brains have been wiped and they've been reprogrammed to work!"

Funny you should call them drones, Garrett had said.

"Barnes has the explosives rigged to go off, and I can't stop it! I've got the workers in an emergency blast chamber, but I don't know if—"

Buck cut her off. "Joella, listen to me—get in that chamber with them and close the door!"

He was shouting now.

"Close the shield door now! You hear me?"

There was no response.

"Joella? Joella!"

"Five meters! Buck," Wilma exclaimed, "we're clear!"

As the glowing warhead appeared over the yawning shaft, Buck pulled back hard on the controls. The tug swung around, rotating to a trajectory away from the moon. The payload barely scraped the edge of the pit, demolishing a catwalk in the process.

Time itself stopped as the tug hovered in its new position.

Then, her main thrusters fired.

There was a flash of light.

Buck and Wilma, with payload in tow, were accelerating towards Saturn.

***

As if answering a mating call, the demolition den produced a flash of light of its own.

Thirty kilometers down, the explosives ignited in sequence, creating a domino effect that built the blast with greater and greater force. Joella covered her head. Barnes simply smiled as oblivion claimed him.

Shaped by the construction of the shaft itself, as well as the dampeners that were in place, the blast shot downwards—fracturing, but not breaking—the moon's mantle. A geyser of water from the subterranean ocean below immediately shot up the shaft and skyrocketed kilometers up into the atmosphere. As the camp's power went off line, the atmospheric shield failed, and the relative warmth of the controlled environment evaporated into space. Exposed to the extreme cold, the ejected water plume flash froze, becoming a corkscrewing crystalline spire—reaching ever upwards insanely towards far Saturn.

***

"I'm sorry, Buck." Wilma said, flatly.

Buck felt nothing. Joella, along with the men whose minds were damaged by that megalomaniacal computer disk, were dead.

He had promised Joella he would protect her, and get her out of this, and he had failed her.

Again.

Buck was numb inside.

The *Canarious*'s comm system was alive with chatter as reports came in from the rest of the camp. Casualties seemed to be limited to those deep within the shaft at the time of the explosion. All the other shuttles had made it clear of the blast zone and the erupting ice geyser. All surface detainees had been safely sheltered within their transportation pods before the blast occurred. Likewise, most security personnel were accounted for. Rescue crews were already in place, recovering survivors. It was only those underground whom had paid the price of Barnes's suicide.

Those underground, Buck lamented, *like Joella...*

Assured his deadly cargo was secure, Buck circled the transport tug around for a better look at the frozen geyser, a monument to yet another loss of human life in the 25th Century. A discoloration in its surface caught his eye—a glint of metal that assumed a familiar shape, embedded in the flash-frozen ice sculpture.

"Wilma," Buck rasped, "coordinates... X34 Y57J." His throat was raw.

As Wilma leaned over him to see out the viewport, he directed her vision toward the new enigma.

"There, in the ice. What do scanners make of that?"

Wilma immediately went to work.

The sensor data merely confirmed his suspicions. It was metal, cylindrical in shape, with twisted unfurled wings that looked all the more like ancient solar panels. "It looks like a probe of some kind," Wilma observed. "Maybe a satellite or message buoy."

Wilma frowned. "It looks ancient, Buck—it must have been buried deep within the ice, probably kilometers down."

But it was the markings on its ventral side that really caught Buck's attention. At first glance, it might resemble the flag of the U.E.D.—United Earth Directorate—several red and white stripes and a field of blue. Except that the Earth Directorate flag had a U.N. symbol in that blue field, and its colored stripes were broken interlocking shapes. No, this flag pre-dated that by at least several hundred years. Its blue field contained an array of stars, and its red and white stripes were straight and true.

Below it were inscribed a few bold words,

UNITED STATES ARK IV.

"Buck," Wilma reached out and touched his hand.

"You look like you've just seen a ghost."

"Yeah," Buck muttered to himself. "I just may have, Wilma." He sat back in the pilot seat, his shoulders heavy.

"I just may have."

***

But Daddy," Ardala asked, "What does it do?"

On Gamma Draconis III, the Princess followed her father Emperor Draco back towards the transport tube that had brought them deep beneath Mt. Draconis.

"It? What 'it,' child?" Having already forgotten what they were talking about, Draco maneuvered his hover platform up the ramp and back into his transient quarters.

"The weapon," Ardala replied, "This *mass collector.*"

As the doors slid shut behind her, Draco activated the controls that would ascend the royal chambers back to their proper place within the palace once more. A steady hum of antigrav machinery replaced the dull echoes of the caverns below. They were moving.

"It..." Draco started, thought about what he was going to say, then flashed a grin. "well, I guess you could say it... moves worlds."

Ardala still didn't understand. Draco sighed, then launched into as technical an explanation as any she'd ever heard from him.

"It is capable of drawing upon the gravity of a local object, such as a planet, star, or moon, and projecting that gravity itself—essentially creating a gravity field of immense size."

"But to what end?" Ardala gasped. *Really, this is getting boring.*

Draco glided to the center of his chambers, leading the charge with his remote in hand. He pressed yet another button, and a large table emerged from the floor. It wasn't just any table, of course, Ardala had seen this one in use before. It was a strategic analysis grid. Updateable from any Star Fortress's computer, the Emperor could access real time or recorded holographic information as he saw fit. As Draco punched in his codes, Ardala noted that he was accessing the *Draconia's* computer banks.

Before them, a hologram of the entire Terran solar system sprang to life, rotating and hovering above the projectors built into the table itself. As the light-show planets lazily circled their star, Draco spoke.

"Tell me, my dear—did your tutors teach you about the other planets in the Earth system?"

Ardala stiffened. "I learned a thing or two."

"Yes, of course you did, my dear," Draco was lost in thought, absorbed by the hologram displayed before him. "Of course you did. Take this world, for instance—the planet Mars." Draco skewered the holographic red planet on his finger. "A lifeless ball of dust. Did you know Mars is named for an ancient earth god of war?"

"Yes, Daddy." Sometimes it was like talking to Buck, except Daddy only seemed to know boring things from the past.

"Let their war god be my weapon of retribution," he smiled.

Ardala was confused. Draco was livid.

"Have the weapon fitted to *Draconia*. Go to their star system." His eyes were wild now, darting to and fro.

"Take that planet, use the weapon's gravity to pull it out of its orbit and put it on a trajectory to smash the Earth itself!"

Draco continued his rant. "Even their much-vaunted defense shield cannot survive a cataclysm of that magnitude." Draco made a mock sad-face, as if he was weeping. "It will simply overload." As he finished, he bared his rotting teeth in a menacing grin.

Certain he had not spoken correctly, Ardala amended him.

"Daddy, you mean *threaten* to smash the Earth—if they don't give us what we want."

Right?

"No," he flatly denied.

No?

Draco's voice was almost a whisper. "No more threats. The time for threats is past."

"As the Earth itself dies, wait, then attack any survivors who flee the planet with all your forces."

"W-without making any demands?" Ardala stammered.

Draco was talking purposeful genocide.

"Kill them all!" he railed at her. "And not like the other times I've sent you to do it. No compromises," he spat.

"No deals!"

He was frothing now. "Wipe out every single living thing on that planet!"

Of course, Draco had ordered the Earth destroyed before.

This time, however, seemed somehow… different.

Ardala involuntarily shrank from the man that had sired her. While the official stance had always been merciless retribution for the Terrans, Draco had always given Ardala carte blanche in handling the situation in the past. The Draconian Empire had crushed many civilizations under their heel, but in all cases they had given a world the chance to surrender. It was one thing to arrive in orbit and incinerate a capital city, then threaten to do the same to the rest of the planet if the inhabitants did not bend to the Draconian way. It was quite another thing to simply annihilate an entire world and then exterminate the remainder of its populace without prejudice.

At least if the first way failed, and you did end up killing them all, they brought it upon themselves.

She had to remind herself how many times the Terrans had been a thorn in her father's side, and how many times she herself had been made to look the fool in front of them. They'd quite simply had their chance to submit a thousand times over and defied the Empire time and time again.

She had to question herself. *Am I becoming… merciful?*

The once and future Emperor noted his daughter's revulsion and regained his composure—at least outwardly. No longer barking like a rabid dog, his plans still bore the mark of genocide—but seasoned with a sprinkling of "survival of the fittest." As if reading her thoughts, he adjusted his logic accordingly.

"Think of the Earth as merely the capital city of our enemy, my dear. When Earth falls, their precious 'Federation' will succumb to us as well." Draco spoke calmly now. "The Empire will take what we need from their worlds and strip them bare." He let her drink that in a moment before delivering his killing stroke.

"Their death will be our life."

Draco maneuvered his platform between Ardala and the hologram of Earth's star system. He paused for effect, his back to his eldest daughter.

"That is, unless you think my plan too harsh, my dear?" Draco dangled the bait. "If you haven't the stomach for it—"

Remembering her twenty-nine sisters packed in the throne room far above, Ardala was quick to bite. "No, Daddy, of course not. I mean, of course I do—"

"Good," he cackled lightly, "good. Because I've chosen you, Ardala; you will be my sword."

The hover bed rotated until Draco was looking her right in the eye. "You," he poked her with his sausage finger, "are now Empress of Draconia."

ACT IV

"Good work, humans, good work!"

Doctor—*Warden* Maximus was positively radiant.

Literally.

The lights in his faceplate were beaming, throwing a green glow across the bay. The warden rode onto the picket cruiser's flight deck perched upon the back of a transport drone, escorted by his two scarlet colored ambuquads. The color clash reminded Wilma of Buck's apartment during the holiday he called Christmas.

Watching the awkward jerky movements of the ambuquads now, Wilma suspected these three drones were not particularly clever—unlike Twiki. Maximus likely had their memory wiped routinely, in order to create workers who knew nothing but their job.

Just like Maximus had done to the men serving in the deep mines, Wilma thought. *If Buck was right, of course.*

She frowned.

Buck was usually right.

There was a lift platform installed on the end of the hangar's catwalk, a slow moving mechanism that would take some time to get the warden situated before those assembled on the actual flight deck below. Wilma took the opportunity to assess the situation.

Aside from Maximus and his robotic entourage, there were several technicians serving the two ruby-winged starfighters in the tiny hangar. Eight security androids accompanied the detainee LeFeatt, and of course, there were Wilma and Buck.

The odds weren't necessarily in their favor, but they'd certainly faced worse. It was clear that the shipment of Archaea was going to be late one way or the other. There were two starfighters sitting right here, ready for launch. They could subdue the androids, steal the ships, rendezvous with a full fighter squadron and troop transport, and be back here in force within six hours.

If they were going to do this, now seemed like the right time.

The only real loose end is the blazium warhead, Wilma pondered. *Can we leave a weapon like that in these incompetent monsters' hands?*

They had only brought it back in the first place because there was no way they were going to fly it out of here with a crane tied around the Canarious transport tug.

Can we still steal it? she considered.

And what about Uma and the security team?

Wilma shot a quick look in Buck's direction; he was clearly angry. As far as he was concerned, Joella had died because he had sent her down into the demolition pit. The Colonel tried to meet his gaze, but Rogers might as well have been in another time and place instead of just from one—staring straight ahead as the mechanized warden descended from above.

He's more than angry, Wilma realized. *Buck is furious.*

"Lieutenant Dex and Officer Mateo." The Warden's voice echoed in the cavernous launch bay. "In recognition of your duty in stopping the detainee LeFeatt from appropriating rehabilitation center property, namely one transport tug equipped with a blazium warhead, preventing his escape from said complex, and for evacuating the warhead before catastrophic damage was occasioned to the ice shelf, I commend you!"

Rehabilitation center property—the Canarious that Buck and I brought to Enceladus in the first place. Maximus seemed to think everything—and everyone—belonged to him.

Now a vibrant yellow, Maximus continued. "While the situation was not resolved before we lost a crane tower, the demolition pit, the work tunnel, a minor number of workers, and a large amount of explosives, after a thorough cost analysis, I am willing to overlook all that, as the blazium warhead itself was saved.

"A very expensive explosive, I assure you," he continued, "one that would have impacted our budget significantly. I am confident we can recover from the loss of the rest." The Warden's lights shifted to a modest rose. "Let it not be said that I am not a kind and reasonable ruler."

The warden addressed Wilma, directly. "Dex, you will now captain your own transport tug. Captain Harris was recovered just within the atmospheric shield, and has experienced severe frostbite for his ineptness. He is resting in the clinic, for now. I assure you he will be put back to work soon—but under your command."

The warden shifted his attention to Buck.

"Officer Mateo, you are promoted to Assistant Security Chief. You will work from the rehabilitation transport ship with Dr. Garrett and myself—no more running around with the misanthropes for you, human."

Each of the ambuquads reached into the compartments on either side of the Warden's transport drone, producing medals.

"Come, kneel before me and receive recognition."

When Buck didn't move, Wilma did, hoping to cover up his indiscretion. As one of the ambuquads clumsily clipped the magnetic medal to Wilma's flight jacket, she forced a smile.

"Thank you, Doctor," she spoke as though muzzled. The self-absorbed quad failed to notice.

"You too, Mateo." Maximus summoned. "Come!"

Buck finally stepped forward, his distant stare replaced with a coprophagous grin.

Uh-oh, Wilma thought.

Instead of kneeling, Buck whirled and delivered a swift roundhouse kick—smashing his boot right into Warden Maximus's faceplate.

The startled robot was flung across the room, skidding across the far wall and landing face down like a clattering frying pan.

For a moment, there was silence. No one moved. Everyone present simply could not believe what they had just witnessed. Maximus's drone guardians were the first to break the quiet.

Baddi-Baddi-Baddi

Then, there was chaos.

Six androids threw themselves on Buck. He made no move to resist, instead catching Wilma's eye and shaking his head "no." She took his lead and stayed undercover, simply acting confused—which wasn't far from the truth. If they were going to run, now was the time.

Why does Buck want me to stand down?

The remaining android guards pulled their blasters and trained them on the detainee—LeFeatt was not going to take this opportunity to try to escape again. The two drones rushed to help their master without looking first, running right into each other and clanking heads before spinning like tops and falling over.

A muffled voice came from the corner of the room, suddenly audible as the Warden raised his own volume to compensate for his vocorder—and face—being pressed against the floor.

"You dare strike me? What is the meaning of this? Are you mad?"

"That's what I'd like to know about you, 'Doctor'! This mission is vital to restoring Earth's ecosystem, and you put it in the hands of convicts?" The guards hauled the now restrained Buck to his feet. "Then you make conditions so deplorable for them that they can't help but sabotage it?"

"These men are undesirables," the upside-down Maximus spoke dismissively to the floor. "They are a drain on all civilization. If the Computer Council had its way, all enemies of the state would simply be put to death. As that is not an option you humans have afforded us, I have found a way to make use of available resources, and put these dregs of society to work for some greater purpose. That is what they are—a resource to be exploited."

"They are still people," Buck spat. "Men and women who were willing to risk their lives to get out of the hell you've put them in. Barnes was even willing to sacrifice the entire detention center population to spare them the fate you have in store for them!"

As serious as the situation was, Wilma couldn't help but smirk: To any outsider, Buck Rogers would appear to be arguing with what amounted to a face-down old fashioned pie dish.

Maximus's drones gingerly clamped onto him with their clumsy pincers, finally flipping the warden right-side up. The lights upon his face were a fierce red.

"You are condoning an attempted mass murder?" Maximus roared from the corner of the room. His tiny speakers struggled to handle the reverb of his voice; his volume was clearly now set way too high. His faceplate sported a spiderweb crack in it, but otherwise the Warden seemed unharmed. His drones lifted him from the floor.

"Of course not," Buck shook his head. "But human beings will do anything to regain their freedom. What you are doing is just pushing them back into a corner, where they have no choice but to lash out."

As he was placed back on his drone-pedestal, Maximus adjusted his loudness and bass to a more standardized, yet still commanding, level. His glow shifted from red to yellow to blue as he regained his composure. "And of course, you think it better to put my kind in jeopardy."

"No," Buck shook his head. "I'm not suggesting that at all. But machines are more resilient than humans and other races—designed for task we simply weren't made to do. Maybe some kind of compromise—"

"Compromise?" Maximus chuckled. "Here is your compromise, human. You feel so much for these detainees? I'm going to let you help them. In fact, you can go excavate the new pit with them." The lights behind his splintered faceplate changed from a placid blue to a deep crimson. "Guards, strip this man of his rank and rights, and throw him in with the labor force!"

As Buck was dragged away, Wilma noticed he hadn't specifically mentioned the so called human "drones" working in the demolitions den, nor Joella. *Not even the ancient satellite,* she mused. *Exactly what are you up to, Captain Rogers?*

Maximus addressed her and the others. "Ha! Let's see how much the detainees like having quality time with one of their former guards!"

It wouldn't be good for Buck, but Wilma had to assume he knew what he was doing. They still had one ace up their sleeve—something that Maximus hadn't figured out yet. LeFeatt's escape attempt had completely demolished one of the crane towers which completed the jammer array, while Barnes's explosion had caused the camp to lose power temporarily. Those two actions combined had created a hole in their jamming network, and Buck and Wilma had exploited it.

A coded message was sent to the Defense Directorate.
The Cavalry was on its way.

***

As most of the guards escorted the deranged Mateo and the new shuttle captain to their destinations, LeFeatt was forced to his knees before the warden's robot perch. With a single blink of his photoreceptors, Maximus magnetized the detainee's electronic shackles to the deck plate before him. The criminal secure, the last two guards stepped away.

"Now," the computerized warden loomed ominously over his subdued charge. "What to do with you, Jean? Maybe it's time for some… special reconditioning." His diodes burned red.

"What are you talking about, Warden?" LeFeatt feigned confusion. "I heard that Barnes was up to no good. I commandeered the tug so I could get the warhead out of there when that crazy Mateo busted me up good. I should get a reward here!"

"Indeed." With a blink from the warden's photoreceptors, an ambuquad clumsily backhanded the kneeling LeFeatt across the face with its metallic red claw.

Clearly, Maximus wasn't having it. "And that's how you so calmly explained it to the shuttle crew—by nearly sending her captain into orbit and choking the life out of her co-pilot?"

"Okay, okay!" Raising his head from the deck, LeFeatt managed to crack a half a smile. "Actually, Warden, rather than what you should do with me, it's more like what I can do for you."

Dr. Maximus was incredulous.

"How is that, human? What could a homicidal maniac like yourself offer me?"

"It was Barnes who was homicidal," LeFeatt corrected him, "...and suicidal. Me? I'm just a thief who wants to free himself and his brother. I was trying to steal a shuttle, not blow up the camp or the detention center."

"Yes, your brother. I had almost forgotten," Dr. Maximus' glow shifted again from red to blue. "Alright human, speak. What can you offer me?"

"First, a deal." Jean LeFeatt countered, "If the information is as useful as I think it will be to you…"

Maximus conceded. "If it is useful, you and your brother are free men. You have my word as an appointee of the Computer Council."

"So he is alive!" LeFeatt was elated. "What, have you had him in isolation this whole time?"

Dr. Maximus avoided the question.

"If your information is as good as you say it is, I promise you will be reunited with him." The computer disk turned a deep shade of mauve. "But if it is not, you will go under the mind scanner for wasting my time…"

"Okay!" LeFeatt stopped him. "Okay… see, there was something odd about this Mateo guy from the beginning. He looked familiar, but I couldn't place him. Then, when they hit me on the transport tug, I thought I heard the woman call him by his first name before I passed out. Except she didn't say Anthony…"

"Go on…" Maximus urged him.

"Well, it wasn't until that little martial arts display that I remembered where I'd seen him before. My brother and I used to work for Jalor LaDavin, and—"

If a machine could sigh, Maximus would have.

"Get to the point, human!"

"See, officially, the guy you just threw in the labor camp is just some celebrity. He's supposed to be 500 years old—and I'm pretty sure he works for the Defense Directorate."

Every light on Dr. Maximus's face turned white. "500 years?! Then, the man that just kicked me…"

"Yup," LeFeatt smiled. "You just caught yourself Buck Rogers."

***

On Gamma Draconis III, deep within Mt. Draconis, the Emperor of Draconia had chosen a successor—and that successor was Ardala.

"Oh, Daddy, you are wonderful, I—"

"Silence, whelp!" Draco snapped. "I saw you falter—saw you show weakness. Do you think your sisters wouldn't also, or did you think I was too far gone to notice? I may be on my deathbed, but I'm not too old and fat to tan your behind!" he roared.

Ardala responded by pouting.

"I've had enough of your pandering, girl." When she continued to pout, Draco's mood softened a bit. Inside, Ardala was amused. Her father always gave in when she pouted.

The Emperor tried a more playful tact with his heir.

"You have what you wanted," he teased.

"Can you keep it, I wonder?"

Properly chastised, Ardala sunk her head.

"That's a good girl." Satisfied he had her attention, Draco guided the hover bed in an approximation of pacing back and forth. "Now, your sisters will not take your appointment easily. They will conspire to exploit any and all weakness you show.

"You have always been my favorite daughter—and Earth has always been your test. But Ardala, my dear, so far you have failed it." He was adamant. "Not this time."

Draco's hover bed glided around his daughter, circling her, moving in for the kill. "You must be ruthless, cunning, merciless—all traits I know you hold well, my dear!"

At that, Ardala lifted her head in pride.

"And," Draco rose his plump index finger, "as per tradition, you must take a husband within one year, a strong man, loyal to the Empire." He stopped the hover platform directly in front of her, and reached out to grasp at her. "Stronger than Kane, Ardala. Ruthless like his younger brother was, or invincible like this ineffable Buck Rogers of yours."

Ardala frowned at that. Try as she might, she already knew Buck would not have her. She would have to set her sights elsewhere.

"Above all, he must be loyal!" Draco proclaimed.

Her father loomed even closer. His cherub face, combined with his sunken eyes and rotting grin made him look all the more like the death's head symbol that emblazoned their Marauder fighter craft.

"A warrior-king with which to sire many heirs!" he shouted with apparent glee.

With a final clank, the chamber stopped ascending, now locked back in place within the palace proper. With a flick of a switch, Draco purged the computer of the information he had just shown her, erasing all evidence that the Empire was facing its own death, and shutting down all the room's monitors. The only copy of that data was now in Ardala's hands—for better or for worse—and the only file that remained on his computer was his final testament, declaring Ardala Empress of Draconia.

"But first, assert your dominance. Invade the Earth Territories," He rasped. "Take what we need! Save—"

His breathing was tight now, fast and uneven.

"Daddy? Daddy!"

Draco's eyes rolled over white, and his arms began to shake.

"Warning," the medical computer called out. "Vital signs unstable. Calling med technicians."

Soon the doors whooshed open, and a team of medtechs, along with Kane, the Vizier, and a troop of bodyguards rushed into the royal chambers. Ardala backed away from her father as her commander came up beside her. Concealing the datastick in her hand, she pretended to lose her balance. As Kane reached out to steady her, she slipped the stick into his palm. Kane looked Ardala in the eyes, and immediately understood. Without glancing at his hand, he simply twitched his mustache once as acknowledgement, and slipped the device into his tunic.

Together, they stood back as the medtechs fought for Draco's life. The Vizier, Pythios, fretted to and fro over his master, muttering to himself and doing his best to look concerned. Ardala was not impressed. It troubled her that this man was the only other Draconian to know the secret of the Empire's woes. It was possible this Pythios would have to meet with an untimely accident—to preserve the Empire, of course.

Despite the medics efforts, Draco soon breathed his last. The Emperor opened his mouth and exhaled a thin ghostly wail of breath that lingered in the room long after his passing.

A lone tear ran down Ardala's cheek, her mascara running after it—a single drop to mourn the man who had fathered her.

Draco was gone.

The doctors would be punished of course, but Ardala decided she would not have them executed—she had in many ways benefited from their ineptitude: true she had lost a father, but she had gained an empire.

An empire on its knees, she reflected, with a slight frown.

The sniveling Vizier approached her, feigning humility. "Princess," he began, "you and your sisters have my deepest condolences. I—"

Ardala cut the man off. "Empress."

"Pardon?" The Vizier stammered.

"You will address me as Empress, *not* Princess." All eyes in the room turned to her at once. "My father has adjudicated me to the throne, you will find Draco's last testament in his computer." She raised her chin in proud. "I am now Empress Ardala."

The Vizier froze, confused. The others in the room—Commander Kane, the medtechs and the bodyguards—all immediately turned to her and dropped to one knee. While her ascendance had not been validated by authentification of the Emperor's last testament as of yet, most Draconians knew better than to risk having *not* bowed to their new leader, rather than having bowed to someone whom they believed was their new leader.

Most Draconians, it seemed, except the Vizier.

Kane led them in salute. "All hail, Empress Ardala, ruler of the Draconian realm!"

"All Hail!" the rest of them echoed.

All.

Except.

The Vizier.

Ardala stared pulsars into Pythios. "Well?" It was not a question, so much an invitation to an execution.

The Vizier suddenly seemed to find himself. Quickly dropping to one knee, the squirming man repeated the chant. "All hail, Empress Ardala!"

Ardala smiled, satisfied—for now. "Vizier, go and tell my sisters of the Emperor's passing." She paused for effect. "After they have a moment to grieve, then inform them of my ascendance to the throne."

Before the Vizier could leave, she raised her hand. "And tell the twins I'm taking Tigerman back," her lips curled devilishly. "*And* I'm keeping Pantherman."

She thought about saying something witty, something that Buck might say. Finally, she decided. "That should get their blood broiling!"

The Vizier hesitated for one second, then bowed, and left the room in a flurry of robes.

She addressed the medtechs next. "Have my father's body prepared for viewing—I want him to look regal, commanding," she stared at her father's bloated corpse. *They have their work cut out for them.* "Have new clothing fashioned for him as well, in the finest silks."

Next, she addressed her second in command—her loyal majordomo.

"Kane, the Empire will mourn the Emperor's passing here on Gamma Draconis for exactly one week. After that time, my coronation will take place—and his remains will be taken to the next sector's capital for tribute. This will be repeated sector by sector, until all citizens of the Empire have had a chance to pay their respects to our fallen lord."

Kane stomped his heel, standing at attention.

"Yes, Empress!"

"And Kane," Ardala barked, turning swiftly. "Prepare the *Draconia* to receive a new weapon. As for now, we mourn my father's passing."

The Empress of the Draconian realm paused, her smile sinister.

"In one week's time," she added, "we head for Earth."

TO bE ConTinUEd...

THE SERIES CONTINUES IN THESE EXCITING PULP NOVELLAS FROM BLAM! VENTURES

BUCK ROGERS IN THE 25TH CENTURY

THE 1979 TV SERIES CONTINUES!

NOVELLA 2

$7.99 US

"WHO MOURNS FOR THEOPOLIS?"

DRACONIAN FIRE: EPISODE 2

ANDREW E.C. GASKA

LOOK FOR BOTH IN 2016

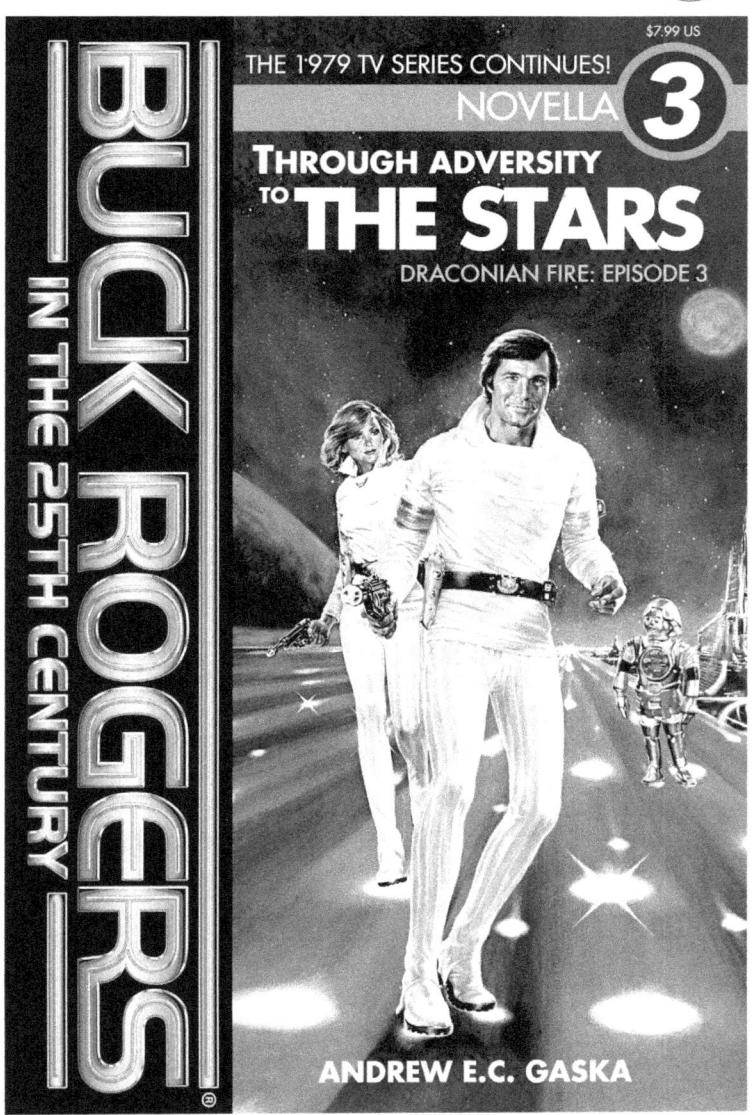

THE 1979 TV SERIES CONTINUES!

NOVELLA 3

THROUGH ADVERSITY TO THE STARS

DRACONIAN FIRE: EPISODE 3

$7.99 US

BUCK ROGERS IN THE 25TH CENTURY

ANDREW E.C. GASKA

GET MORE INFO AT **FACEBOOK.COM/BUCKROGERSSEASON3**

BLAM! Ventures

Founded by CEO and Creative Director Andrew E. C. Gaska, BLAM! Ventures is a full service guerrilla design studio that produces high quality multimedia entertainment.

In creating BLAM! Ventures, Gaska sought to bring a cinematic scope to sequential storytelling, be it in comics, animation, or more, with the intention of reaching a broader and more diverse audience than ever before. While holding fast to the ideal of the old aesthetics, BLAM! Ventures pushes onward to a thrilling new dynamic in sequential art, giving the creator the freedom to explore their utmost boundaries, while providing the reader/viewer with something to eagerly anticipate. With a meticulous attention to detail, the team at BLAM! Ventures believes that all things should serve the story, from art to dialogue, coloring to lettering, voice overs to sound effects, and everything else between the gutters.

In addition to its in-house productions, BLAM! develops both original and licensed properties for its clients, creating full packages ready to be taken to a publisher. Specializing in illustrated prose and comic and sequential art storytelling, along with digital downloadable services, BLAM! Ventures offers up both an eclectic lineup of talent and an exciting array of possibilities.

BLAM! Ventures titles have been released through Eisner Award winning publishers Archaia Entertainment and BOOM! Studios, soon to be joined by Titan Comics and Magnetic Press.

In association with our publishing partners, BLAM! Ventures' books include the graphic novels Critical Millennium™: The Dark Frontier and Charger™. Our ever growing library of Retrograde™ imprint titles include the illustrated novel Conspiracy of the Planet of the Apes® and the graphic novels Space:1999® Aftershock and Awe and Classic Space:1999®: To Everything That Was. Those titles will soon be joined in 2016 by The illustrated novels Buck Rogers in the 25th Century®: Draconian Fire and Killer, with more on the way!

To find out more, visit *blamventures.com*

@blamventures

facebook.com/blamventures

About the Author

Andrew E.C. Gaska is an author, digital artist, producer and art director. A franchise consultant for Twentieth Century Fox, he has also served as a freelance consultant for the past fifteen years to Rockstar Games on such hit titles as *Grand Theft Auto III-V*, *Red Dead Redemption*, the *Midnight Club* series, and all other major releases. He is the founder and creative director of BLAM! Ventures, a guerrilla design studio that produces integrated media for the comic book and science fiction industry. His comic and prose work include the sci-fi graphic novel Critical Millennium™: the Dark Frontier and comic series Hawken®: Melee from Archaia Entertainment/BOOM! Studios, as well as the Space:1999™ graphic novel series and the illustrated novel Conspiracy of the Planet of the Apes®, all produced by BLAM!

He is currently working on the Buck Rogers® novella and hardcover series, a number of creator owned comic series, an H.P. Lovecraft graphic novel adaptation titled Madness™, and a new classic Planet of the Apes® novel series from Titan Books.

Drew resides beneath a mountain of action figures in New York with his gluttonous feline, Adrien. Adrien often perches atop this pinnacle of plastic, proclaiming himself 'lord of the figs.'

Drew humors him.

CPSIA information can be obtained
at www.ICGtesting.com
Printed in the USA
BVHW071428140819
555860BV00024B/1911/P

9 781523 712496